SOLD OUT

Dedicated to my brothers and their wives: Eddie and Dionisia, Kenny and Mary, Alan and Linda, and Earl and Annette. I love all of you!

ZONDERkidz

Sold Out
Copyright © 2007 by G Studios, LLC

Requests for information should be addressed to:
Zonderkidz, *Grand Rapids, Michigan 49530*

Library of Congress Cataloging-in-Publication Data

Crouch, Cheryl, 1968-

Sold out / by Cheryl Crouch.

p. cm. -- (Chosen Girls ; bk. 6)

"G Studios."

Summary: Trin, tries to prove her worth to her missing father by staging the biggest and best talent show that James Moore has ever seen, but her pride gets in the way.

ISBN-13: 978-0-310-71272-5 (softcover)

ISBN-10: 0-310-71272-6 (softcover)

[1. Talent shows--Fiction. 2. Bands (Music)--Fiction. 3. Schools--Fiction. 4. Pride and vanity--Fiction. 5. Christian life--Fiction.] I. Title.

PZ7.C8838So 2007

[Fic]--dc22

2007022883

Editor: Bruce Nuffer
Art direction and design: Sarah Molegraaf
Interior composition: Christine Orejuela-Winkelman and Melissa Elenbaas

Printed in the United States of America

07 08 09 10 11 12 • 10 9 8 7 6 5 4 3 2 1

SOLD OUT

By Cheryl Crouch

ZONDERVAN.com/
AUTHORTRACKER
follow your favorite authors

Oh **wow,** I'm getting used to how quiet Mello is. It doesn't bug me anymo

BE ON TV!

We're looking for a band to star
in our new ad campaign

Contact:

pizza pete's

headquarters for more information

How I'll spend the money from Pizza Pete's .

☑ Shoes!!!

☑ Sandals, boots
(brown and black), slides — pink.

New running shoes?!?!

☑ Jeans or cropped pants — mayb

POW!

$35.99

in fact, I've decided it's nice to have a friend who listens sometimes. _ello's the kind of person who REALLY listens, because she cares what you're saying. **Nice.** Way nice.

pride* *insecurity

This talent show is going to be the best ever! James Moore has never had a leader who wanted to do this right. With the Chosen Girls singing the finale, everyone will know it is way cool to be

in this talent show. And I will make sure everyone

knows that **Trin** Adams is revolutionizing it this year.

Those who walk in pride he is able to humble.
—Daniel 4:37

Cooper's Copies

CHK 3484   4:47PM   GST 2

3000 copies
at $0.10 per copy
(one sided, black)

Subtotal
Amt Paid $300
                                              $330

cut. Oh wow, I don't know. It's been long forever!!! You know? But maybe a change would help. People always notice when you change some-thing, and they practically have to compliment you if you do something drastic like whack off a foot of hair. Because, please, it's not like they can pretend not to notice, and who'd be rude enough to actually say they didn't love it? Ok I know who. Makayla.

REVOLUTION!
james moore
Talent Show

Like You've Never Seen it Before!

FRIDAY 8 p.m.

AUDITORIUM

Don't miss the dynamic exhibition that's aready gotten the attention of local TV and radio stations.

For More Information, Contact Trin Adams

smile

to*do

- ☑ Get supplies for signs
- ☑ Print more flyers???
- ☑ <u>Practice for grand finale</u>
- ☑ Call Latisha
- ☑ Call Hunter and Harsha

~~Call Makayla~~

-yrics

who am I? That you would love me so
    when you are so far ~~away~~ above me, oh
    I am small, and you are everything
    Your love, it just makes me wanna sing

Jesus, help me see what you see
    when – you – look – at – me

(repeat this)

    I know I am far from wonderful
    I give up and find that **that's** when you'll
    Pick me up in loving arms again
    Make ~~us~~ me <u>wonder</u> where on earth **I've** been

Jesus, help me see what you see
    when – you – look – at – me

Jesus, help me be what you see
    when – you – look – at – me

everything
~~fling~~
~~bling~~
sing ~~sting~~
~~ring~~

LOVE

HARDWARE HOUSE
****
CHK 178   8:01PM   GST 9
****

wooden stakes	1.00
@ 4/$1	
Rope	
@ .12/foot	
30ft	3.60
hammer	4.50
Subtotal	$9.10
Tax 6%	$0.55
Amt Paid	$9.65

know what makes me crazy? Disorganized

people. Wait, that's not true. If it was, I so could

not be friends with Harmony. I guess it just makes

me crazy when disorganized people try to be in

charge of stuff (please!). Especially if I'm supposed

to help make whatever happen, but the poor person

I'm helping is beyond clueless. It's so much easier

to just BE in charge than to help, sometimes.

Ok, most

the time.

Fine —

all the

time???

chapter • 1

...

Friday

I can't believe how fast Mello and Harmony became my best-ever friends after I moved to California. Of course, starting our own band definitely helped. The Chosen Girls have had so many crazy experiences together—that stuff makes for way serious bonding.

It's cool because it feels like I've known them forever, instead of just a year. Sometimes I wish they knew me as well as I know them, and sometimes I'm glad they don't. I mean, they know me. They just don't know everything about me. Like, that my family isn't the perfect family they think we are. It's not like my friends couldn't handle the truth—maybe I'm the one who can't deal.

...

I leaned across the cafeteria table and asked, "So we're meeting at the tryouts, right?"

"*Sí*," Harmony answered. "Four thirty. That should give us time to warm up."

Mello tapped the edge of the table. "I wonder how many bands will show."

Jasmine, a friend from church sitting at the next table, turned around and said, "Couldn't help overhearing. What are you trying out for?"

"Pizza Pete's wants a band for their new ad campaign," I explained.

Jasmine looked starstruck. "That is so awesome. Do you Chosen Girls even *know* how cool you are?"

"We have a pretty good idea," Harmony said, grinning then ducking to avoid the wadded-up napkin Mello chucked at her.

"So will the ads, like, be on TV?" Jasmine asked.

Makayla's voice came from behind me. "Yes, they'll be on TV, and the Makayla Simmons band can't wait to star in them."

I saw Makayla, the self-appointed leader of the Snob Mob, standing between tables with a tiny girl I didn't recognize.

"So you're trying out too?" I asked, forcing my mouth into a smile.

Makayla flung her short silvery-blonde hair. "A formality. I don't know why *anyone else* should bother showing up."

"Are you the Chosen Girls?" asked the girl with Makayla.

I said, "Yeah, hi. What's your name?"

The petite girl grinned shyly and said, "I'm Reesie." Even though her hair and eyes were still the same mousy brown, her whole face seemed to glow when she smiled.

Makayla huffed in obvious disgust. "Reesie, this is Harmonica," she said with a shrug in Harmony's direction. "That's Melodious, and you're speaking to Trendy."

"That's what Makayla calls us," I said. "The rest of the world knows us as Harmony, Mello, and Trin. Are you new at James Moore?"

She nodded. "New to California too. Just moved here from Oregon."

"You'll love it," Mello offered. "There's so much to—"

Makayla held onto her empty lunch tray with one hand and grabbed Reesie's elbow with the other. "Yeah, well, she's not looking for things to do or for new friends. But since she's my new bass player, it's probably good she met the 'other' band. Not that you're any *real* competition."

I bit my lip to keep from pointing out how many times our band has left hers in the dust. It didn't matter, because Harmony blurted, "Unless you count the channel 34 contest and the Hopetown Battle of the—"

"Yeah, let's talk about the Battle of the Bands," Makayla agreed. "The *L.A.* Battle of the Bands."

Harmony rolled her eyes in frustration.

I whispered, "It's just Makayla, Harmony. Let it go."

Reesie pulled away from Makayla and asked, "Which of you plays bass?"

Harmony lifted her hand. "I do."

"I hear you're fantastic," Reesie offered. "Maybe we could jam sometime."

Makayla snorted. "I'm sure Harmony could learn a thing or two from you, Reesie. She's got plenty of room for improvement."

"You must not think she's too bad, since you begged her to join *your* band," I reminded Makayla.

Reesie completely ignored our exchange. "So what else are you into?"

Harmony pretended to snap a picture. "I'm a photographer for the yearbook. And I make jewelry." She jangled the bracelet on her wrist.

"She's also a blue belt in karate," Mello added proudly.

Makayla put her hand to her face. "Ooh! I'm so scared."

Reesie nodded. "Cool. What about you, Mello?"

Mello shrugged. "I'm the drummer. And I do layouts for the yearbook."

"She designs purses too," I said, holding up the one Mello made just for me.

"That's hideous," Makayla said, wrinkling her pug nose. "It's the exact same shade of pink as your hair."

Reesie reached out to touch the satiny fabric. "I love it. How do I get one?"

Harmony whipped out one of our little business cards. She handed it to Reesie as the bell rang, and everyone started picking up trays and filling the aisles. I stood up and grabbed mine.

"I didn't get to find out much about you, Trin," Reesie apologized. "Maybe next time. Right now, Makayla's going to show me where my next class is."

"There's nothing to know about Trin," Makayla told her as they inched toward the tray return. Even though she faced away from me, I could hear Makayla's voice clearly.

"I don't know why Trin acts like she's so great," Makayla continued. "If Harmony and Mello hadn't felt sorry for her and taken her in when she moved here, she'd be an absolute nobody. She's just a new girl who sings in the Chosen Girls, and that's it. Except for the band, she's a nobody."

I slammed my tray back onto the table. "The new girl?" I yelled. "A nobody? I've been here a whole year!"

Mello and Harmony looked at each other like, *Uh-oh.*

"Is that what people at this school think of me? That I'm the new girl who sings for Chosen Girls and *that's it*?"

Harmony leaned across the table. "It's just Makayla, Trin. Let it go."

"Did you guys really feel sorry for me?" I asked, dropping back into my seat as Makayla's words sunk in. "Is that why you're my friends?"

"Right, Trin," Mello answered. "There's something about you that brings out our natural feelings of pity. Maybe it's the fact that you're drop-dead gorgeous and always dressed like a runway model."

"Or it could be your outgoing personality," Harmony added.

Mello grinned. "No, I think it's your amazing voice and the way you make an electric guitar sing. Poor Trin."

"You're so pitiful we had to force ourselves to take you in," Harmony finished. She reached across the table to give my shoulder a squeeze, then she and Mello picked up their stuff and joined the crowd waiting to turn in trays. I made myself follow them, but I didn't join in their conversation about Reesie and how someone so nice could have ended up in Makayla's band.

As I put my tray on the conveyor belt and watched it disappear, I thought, *What if everyone in the school thinks like Makayla? There is more to me than singing in our band. The time has come for me to show the people of James Moore what I'm made of.*

• • •

That afternoon, I sat in science, trying to listen but unable to stop thinking about Makayla and what I could do to prove myself to her—something that would show the whole school who I am.

When my phone vibrated in my pocket, I clicked into my inbox to find the text message:

Hi, honey. Sorry it's been so long since I've written. I may be in your area two weeks from now, and I'd like to come see you if I can work it out. Love, Jake

As soon as I saw his name, I felt that same mixed-up feeling I get every time he decides to write. Excited, angry, hopeful ... sad. How can one person make me feel all that?

I guess that's the power a father has. Especially one who walks out on you when you're just four years old.

I didn't reply to his message in class. I knew better than to try that. Mrs. Lewis would take up my phone in a flash. I didn't want to end up explaining to everybody in science about Jake. I hadn't even told Harmony and Mello about Mom's divorce and that my biological father lived in Colorado. It didn't seem necessary, since my mom's new husband, Jeff Adams, adopted me when I turned seven. For all anyone in Hopetown knew, we were a perfect family.

My real father's leaving was ancient history and had nothing to do with my life now.

Besides, for some stupid reason, his messages usually make me cry.

So I spent the rest of class worrying about Jake's text message *and* what Makayla said. I didn't learn a thing about the periodic table. Just a bunch of letters and numbers up there on the wall.

When the bell rang I rushed to a bathroom stall. I stood there and held my phone for a while, trying to convince myself I didn't care what Jake had to say. So he was my "real" dad. So, even now, I could remember each word of the goofy lullaby he sang to me every night. And the spicy smell of his aftershave when I kissed him good-bye every morning.

Until that one morning, when I woke up and he wasn't there.

Did those memories give him the right to barge in on my life when I hadn't heard from him for two years?

I'd like to come see you.

Did he mean it? He always promised to come, but he never showed.

What if he really came this time? Would it be good or bad for him to visit me in Hopetown?

I left the bathroom and pushed through the crowded hall. I thought about my friends he'd never met and events we'd won that he didn't know about. Would he be impressed with my life here? What would he think of California? Of the Chosen Girls?

More important, what would my father think of me?

• • •

I sat by my friend Latisha Punch during math. Latisha started talking about her work for student council the minute the bell rang for the end of class.

"They gave me the talent show this year!"

"Ohwow!" I answered as I gathered up my books. "Latisha, that's awesome."

She widened her brown eyes in horror. "Hello, girlfriend?" she said. "You might as well carry a sign that says, 'Kick me. I'm new.'"

"Huh?" I asked. "What do you mean?"

She rolled her eyes as we headed into the crowded hall. "The talent show at James Moore is famous, Trin. Famous for being way, way beyond lame. It stinks. It's stupid and boring, and nobody who's anybody wants to come within a hundred yards of it. Weren't you here during last year's talent show?"

"I don't remember hearing about one," I answered.

She nodded. "There ya go."

"It can't be that bad," I insisted.

"The winner did a juggling act."

I thought about it. "Juggling can be cool."

Latisha shook her head. "Not when the person is only juggling two balls. And still manages to miss half the time."

I laughed out loud. "You're kidding. That was the winning act?"

"It's not funny," she said, maneuvering us around a group of chatting cheerleaders. "The runner-up played a solo. You know that old song 'You Light Up My Life'?"

"Sure," I answered with a giggle. "It's a classic."

"Well, it doesn't sound so classic when it's played on the kazoo. I'm telling you, the show reeks."

"But Latisha, if you're in charge, you can change all that," I told her. "Wouldn't it be fun to make it a huge success?"

"And just how do you suggest I do that?" she asked, as we stopped outside her next class. "And don't say, 'By letting the Chosen Girls be in it.' It's strictly amateur."

"Wait," I said, leaning against the door frame. "When is it?"

"In just two weeks," she answered with a groan.

"What if my band did a grand finale kind of thing? Like while the judges tally the scores."

Her face lit up. "Would you really? You'd do that for me? Don't say it if you don't mean it. Because, Trin, I'm telling you, I think if a big-name band like yours got involved, it might get other people interested. Maybe we could even get on the news or something!"

The warning bell rang. "I've gotta go," I said. "But count on the Chosen Girls. And count on me too."

"Thanks, Trin," she yelled after me. "I'm so stoked. You're saving me from social suicide. Finally, it won't just be the nobody show."

As I rushed down the hall, Latisha's words echoed in my head. Maybe I could help her out and help myself at the same time. I knew I could make the talent show off-the-charts amazing.

Then Makayla will know I'm not a nobody, I thought. *I won't be "the new girl who's in Chosen Girls." I'll be Trin Adams, whose leadership skills transformed the show—and the whole school—into something to be proud of.*

And if my real father happens to visit during the talent show and get blown away by the way-fabulous job his daughter did on it, well, that won't hurt, either.

chapter • 2

•••

Still Friday

Harmony, Mello, and I warmed up with six other bands in a makeshift practice room at Pizza Pete's headquarters.

Lamont, our sound guy, walked in nervous circles around us. "I wish they'd let me run sound for your audition. Why don't people understand how vital sound is? I'm sick of being treated like an optional feature."

I looked up from my electric guitar. "We recognize how valuable you are, Lamont. If we get a contract, we'll write you in. But give these people a break. They sell pizzas, not CDs."

"Good point," he answered, satisfied for the moment.

A worker stuck her head in the door and read from a clipboard: "Next up, Off and Running. Then the Cranberry Canaries, followed by Chosen Girls."

"About how long?" Harmony asked.

"I'd say we're running ten minutes per band," the woman answered before she stepped out.

Harmony let her bass hang by the strap around her neck as she grabbed her stomach. "Twenty minutes? Then we have to audition, and then pack up. It'll be at least an hour until we can eat, and I'm starving."

"What about the peanut butter cups you just ate?" I asked.

Lamont said, "You had peanut butter cups? Don't you know they come in sets because you're supposed to share them?"

"You'd think they'd have free pizza or something," Mello suggested, still tapping on the drums. "We *are* at their headquarters."

"*Si! Muy bueno*, Mello. How can we sing about their pizza if we don't get to eat it? I don't think it's morally right to pro- mote a product unless I believe in it." She yelled, "I need to speak to a manager! Who's in charge here?"

Mello punched her. "Don't blow our chance. This would be a great gig for us."

Lamont said, "Yeah, Harmony, save your complaints until *after* you get a contract."

"What did you say, Mello?" I said. "You mean you're really OK with being on TV this time?"

She shrugged and grinned. "It would be a great gig. Besides, Harmony's just being a twit. She eats Pizza Pete's pizza at least once a week."

Harmony raised her eyebrows. "But maybe they changed the recipe since last Friday. You never know with these big corporations."

I laughed. "Well, whether or not we get the pizza deal, we're OK," I said. "I got the hookup for a gig in a couple weeks ... and Lamont, we'll definitely need you."

"Where? When?" Harmony asked.

"We're the grand finale for the James Moore talent show."

Their mouths dropped open, and they stared at me like wax figures in a museum.

"Way cool, huh?" I continued. "I mean, I know we can't compete since we're, like, professionals. So I signed us up to do a song or two while the judges figure the scores. I want us to do something amazing, with our own backdrop and maybe even special effects. Something everyone will talk about—"

Mello was the first one to regain the power of speech and movement. "Oh, Trin, no! Not the James Moore talent show. That's just not an option."

"Right," Harmony agreed. She came close enough to put her hands on my shoulders. Her bass bumped my electric as she looked deep into my eyes and said, "If you have any respect for the Chosen Girls, you'll take our name off that list immediately."

Lamont looked at his watch. "I bet the school building is still open. Where's the list, Trin? I'll run and scratch your name right now."

I took a step back and looked at them. "Come on! It's a simple school talent show. Why is everyone so freaked out?"

Lamont shook his head. "Trin, I've been homeschooled my whole life, and yet even I know how pathetic the James Moore talent show is. Does that tell you anything?"

"The sign-up sheet reads like a 'Who's Who' of dweebs," Mello added. "The only reason *anyone* goes is to laugh at people who are so out of touch they don't know they're being laughed at."

"But it doesn't have to be that way," I insisted. "Other schools have way cool talent shows."

Lamont ran a hand over his curly, super-short hair in frustration. "Other schools have basketball players who go straight to the NBA too. That doesn't mean it's going to happen at James Moore."

I held my ground. "Our school deserves a chance. Who made the rule that the show has to be lame?"

"I think it was etched in stone about the same time Moses got the Ten Commandments," Harmony answered.

"We're wasting time. Just go, Lamont. Please," Mello begged. "Find the list and take our name off. And don't put a wimpy little line through it. Blot it out completely. Make sure no one can tell it was ever there."

I stepped in front of Lamont. "It's not that easy."

"Why?" they all three asked at the same time.

"I didn't write our name on a list. I promised Latisha we'd sing. She's in charge this year, and she's counting on us."

Harmony threw her hands in the air. "That's it, then. We're doomed. Our fate is sealed."

Mello covered her face with her hands. "This is awful. I should have known something like this would happen. Every time it looks like we're doing OK ..."

Lamont just looked at me, slowly shaking his head.

"Look, there is no need to panic. This year's show is going to be way fabulous," I promised. "Everyone's going to love it. The whole school will be blown away, and people who aren't in it are the ones who will feel stupid."

"And what is going to make the difference?" Harmony asked. "You think our closing song can revolutionize over fifty years of humility and shame?"

"James Moore hasn't even been a school for fifty years," I reminded her. "And yes, I think our song will help. So does

Latisha. She said if we're in the show, other cool people will sign up. But that's not all." I swallowed before I declared, "I'm going to do whatever it takes to make this talent show a huge success."

"Like what?" Harmony asked.

I shrugged. "Well, I'm not sure exactly. Not yet. But I'll think of something."

"Maybe she's right," Lamont said, tilting his head and looking at me. "Maybe it is time for a change. If anyone could pull it off, Trin could."

Before I could say thank you, Mello said, "Yeah. You can say that, Lamont, because you don't go to school there. You won't have to walk the halls and listen to everyone laugh at you all day, every day, for the rest of your—"

"Wait," Harmony interrupted. "Trin messed up. We all acknowledge that. But apparently we're stuck with her mistake. Let's think about this logically. If we can't get out of the show, we've got to work together and do what Trin's talking about. Somehow we've got to make the show a success."

"But *I'm* going to do that," I reminded her. "I *want* to. I didn't mean you all had to—"

"So let's start at the beginning. Why is the show always a disaster?" Lamont asked.

"The acts," Mello answered. "A talent show is supposed to showcase talent. Apparently James Moore has none."

"Or the people with talent won't sign up," I said.

"I've got it!" Harmony shouted. "We know the cool, talented people would never sign up to be in the show. But what if we got them to be on staff? They could coach the people who try out—you know, help them tweak their acts."

Lamont stroked his chin. "Hmm. Might be a good chance for them to strut their stuff."

"And if they're part of making the show happen, they won't make fun of it," Mello added.

I nodded. "Sounds good. But do you think anyone will agree to do it?"

Harmony looked shocked. "What? Of course they will. When they hear the Chosen Girls are involved, they'll rush to be a part of it. That's what you're counting on, right?"

I nodded and got out my phone. "Right. OK, I'm calling Latisha."

Mello grabbed a chunk of her hair in each hand, as if she wanted to pull it out. "Now? This is not the time to chat on the phone, Trin! Our audition is coming up any second."

I stepped away from Mello. Latisha answered right away. "You're backing out, aren't you? I knew once you started talking to people you'd change your mind."

I laughed. "No, Latisha. The Chosen Girls are in, just like I promised. And I have a great plan to make the rest of the show better."

Harmony pointed to herself, mouthing the words, "My idea. Mine." I waved her off and told Latisha about having student coaches.

"I love it!" Latisha gushed. "But how will we get them to volunteer?"

"You leave that to me," I said. "I'll find a way to get people excited. You just get ready to be known as the person who revolutionized James Moore. And listen, I've got some great people in mind to help."

"Why don't you let me think about that, Trin? I'd like to choose the workers, since I'll be dealing with them for a couple weeks straight."

I tried to keep the disappointment out of my voice. "Well, sure. I just thought, if you wanted me to recruit them and all — but yeah, that's fine."

The Pizza Pete's worker stepped through the door. "Chosen Girls, you're on."

"Gotta go, Latisha."

I followed Harmony, Mello, and Lamont down the hall and into the tryout room. A row of people sat in folding chairs — a man in a suit, a woman in a bright orange polo with the Pizza Pete's logo embroidered on the pocket, and a couple of college students in Pizza Pete's T-shirts. They munched on cold pizza slices and looked bored.

Harmony said, "Please say if you like us you'll give me a slice of pizza!"

They laughed and sat up a little straighter. We smiled at each other and at the judges and started our song.

It went great.

They did offer us pizza afterward, and we stood around and chatted for a few minutes. Finally, the monitor stuck her head in and said, "Hey, I've got three more bands out here."

The man in the suit said, "I guess we've got to listen to them, huh?" He didn't sound like he wanted to.

The woman in the orange shirt sighed. "I suppose. But we've sure enjoyed talking with you, Chosen Girls. You have a wonderful sound."

"Yeah. You rock," one of the college kids added.

"And *you* have wonderful pizza!" I answered. "Thanks for sharing."

In the hall, Harmony said, "We so have this in the bag!"

"They're, like, our best friends now," Mello added.

Lamont smiled. "Good job. You're naturals."

"Celebrating a little early, aren't you?" Makayla asked, stepping out of the practice room and into the hall.

"Hi, Makayla. I thought maybe your band wasn't going to show," I said.

Makayla followed us into the room where we loaded our instruments back into their cases. She said with a smirk, "We're trying out last. And we're going to be so good, they'll forget every other band they heard today."

I looked into Makayla's steely gray eyes.

"You sound pretty confident," I said.

"I have a reason to be," she answered.

"Then let's make a deal. If you get the contract, the Chosen Girls will—" I saw a bright orange Pizza Pete's shirt passing in the hall. "We'll wear T-shirts to school that say, 'The Makayla Simmons band rocks.'"

I heard Mello and Harmony gasp.

Makayla laughed an evil little laugh. "I can't wait to see that!"

"Of course if we get the contract, your band has to wear shirts that say, 'Chosen Girls rock.'"

"I'm not scared."

"For a week!" I added, just to show I wasn't scared either.

"Deal," Makayla said, sticking her hand out to shake on it.

When we walked out a few minutes later, Mello whispered, "The talent show, the T-shirts—how many more potentially humiliating experiences do you have planned for the near future, Trin?"

"Oh, please. You know the judges adored us," I insisted. "Try to tell me you don't love the idea of the Snob Mob wearing Chosen Girls shirts to school."

Harmony's eyes lit up behind her star-shaped glasses. "I'll be sure to have the yearbook camera ready," she said.

I nodded. "That's the spirit. Just stick with me, Chosen Girls, because I'm going to make sure we are looking good. The all-new talent show, the regional ad campaign — Trin Adams has got everything under control."

chapter • 3

...

Sunday

I called a meeting early Sunday afternoon at the shed. A long
time ago the shed was just a garage in Mello's backyard,
but to me it's always been like a little house that's all for us.
It's our favorite place to jam or just hang—it even has cool
botanical prints on the walls and comfy furniture.

Lamont, Harmony, and Mello sat on the squishy tan couch
and looked up at me.

"OK. Our backdrop has to be way fabulous," I told them.
"But something we can set up fast."

"Won't there already be a backdrop for the talent show?"
Mello asked, leaning back and propping her feet up on the
coffee table. "Why do we have to make one?"

I paced in front of them. "Because our act is the grand
finale. I want people to be blown away from the second
the curtain opens on us. I want them talking about me—I
mean the show—for weeks afterward. If nothing else comes

together—which, of course, it will—then our song will be the redeeming factor that saves the whole evening. It's got to be breathtaking."

I caught my breath. "Ohwow, that little *speech* was breathtaking. So, Lamont, can you help us with special effects?"

Harmony picked up a magazine and started flipping through it. "This is a school talent show, Trin, not a Broadway musical."

I made an *L* with my thumb and pointer finger and held it in front of Harmony. "That is exactly the kind of loser attitude that's ruined the show in the past," I said.

"Are you calling me a loser?" asked Harmony.

"No, I'm saying—"

"You think it's my fault the James Moore Talent Show always tanks?"

I groaned in frustration. "No, Harmony. But we've got to change the way we think about it. Completely. This talent show is my chance to—" I stopped. I felt the heat rise in my face as I realized I almost said too much.

Or was it time to tell them? Should I tell them why I needed to prove myself to the rest of the school? But they just laughed when Makayla said that rude stuff about me. They didn't understand how her words ripped apart who I thought I was.

Confident, fun, successful. That's me. Not just some new girl who can't do anything.

"Your chance to what, Trin?" Lamont asked.

I looked at him and then at my two best friends. Forget Makayla and everyone at school. Maybe this would be a good time to tell them the whole truth: That I desperately needed something, anything, to prove my worth to my real father, who didn't even love me enough to stick around. To convince him I was worth the time it took to write, or call, or visit.

To convince myself I was worth it.

"Well, I don't know if it will make sense to you …" I began. I could feel my eyes tearing up.

Harmony dropped the magazine, leaned forward, and put her elbows on her knees. Mello's bright eyes looked deeply into mine. Lamont nodded encouragingly.

I swallowed. "I promised Latisha," I finally said. "I really want to help her. And help our school."

"That's cool," Lamont said.

Mello smiled. "You have a heart of gold, Trin."

Harmony got up and rummaged around. "Mello, where's some paper? And pens or paint or something? We've got to get started."

At that moment I loved my friends more than ever. Even without knowing my whole embarrassing story, they backed me up.

"So what should this thing look like?" Mello asked, pulling paper and pens from some shelves and handing them to Harmony. "Here, you're the designer."

"Of clothes and jewelry," Harmony corrected, dropping onto the couch. "But I'll give it a try. How about something like this?" She leaned over the coffee table and started sketching.

Thirty minutes later we had the design for two multicolored papier-mâché columns with a Chosen Girls sign that spanned the space between them. We split up to gather supplies.

Mello got newspaper, flour, and water from her house. Harmony grabbed a set of poster paints, and I found some plastic tubs. We met in Mello's backyard, and Lamont showed up with chicken wire. All he said was, "Don't even ask."

"I have to ask," Harmony said. "You just happen to have four rolls of chicken wire at your house?"

"OK, I'll tell you. This is the upside of having a dad who never gets rid of anything. It's left over from the time he built rabbit fencing around the garden," he answered.

"You have a garden?" I asked.

Lamont shook his head. "Not since I was five."

Harmony smiled. "Hey, you never know when four rolls of chicken wire might come in handy."

Lamont formed one roll of the wire into a column about six feet tall. "What do you think?"

"It needs to be bigger," I answered.

They looked at me.

I pointed to the other rolls. "Come on. He's got loads of this stuff. I'm sure his mom wants it out of the house. Think big, everybody. We can double that, can't we, Lamont?"

We did, but we had to go outside to do it. When we had two twelve-foot columns, we taped newspaper pages around them. Then we mixed the flour and water into a cream-colored goop that filled three plastic tubs. Lamont tore newspaper pages into long strips, and we dipped them before slapping them onto our giant columns.

I grabbed a couple strips of paper and plunged them into the mix. "So, Lamont, how about some pyrotechnics?"

He laughed.

I carried my dripping paper to the column. "I'm serious."

"Trin, that stuff costs money." He kept tearing strips of paper as if he had settled the issue.

I took two more pieces. "And our band has money."

Harmony pressed her dripping papers onto the columns and asked, "This is going to make me sound stupid, but what are pyrotechnics?"

"Fireworks," Mello answered, picking strips off Lamont's paper pile. "And Trin, no way are we doing them as part of our act."

"Why not?" I asked.

She dunked her papers into the tubs. "The talent show is *inside*, Trin. Have you forgotten that? And I know you promised Latisha something wonderful, but I don't think it's fair to the other acts if we completely blow them away."

"I'm not talking about Fourth of July, two-hundred-feet-in-the-sky fireworks," I explained. "More like a few sparkles to liven things up. Please, Lamont. Think how cool it would be. Wouldn't everyone go crazy-wild? I'm sure there's never been anything like it at James Moore."

He grinned. "It would make an impression," he admitted. "Let me do a little research."

The columns stood drying in the sun, and we had just unrolled a huge strip of poster paper when my phone rang "New York, New York," the song I had plugged in for Latisha.

"Are you still up for being part of the talent show?" she asked.

"Am I up for it?" I watched Mello and Harmony sketching our logo across the poster paper. "I'm working on an awesome backdrop for our closing number as we speak. And I'm planning something else way fabulous."

"Excellent," she answered. "But will you be too busy getting the Chosen Girls ready to help with the rest of the show?"

I handed the container of poster paints to Lamont and pointed to the poster. "Of course not!"

"Well then, I've been thinking about this a lot. Trin, I'd like to officially ask you to be in charge of publicity."

"Publicity? Oh. Um, sure. I can do that," I mumbled.

"And I want you to be my helper ... with the whole show," she said.

I smiled. "Ohwow, yes! Thanks. You won't be sorry, Latisha."

"Great."

"Hey, Latisha, this is a small thing ..." I began.

"Yeah?"

I walked away from the others and dropped my voice. "Can you call it something else besides 'helper'? Like, maybe, assistant coordinator or publicity manager or something?"

She laughed. "Sure, Trin. You pick your title, and we'll go with it. Do you want to hear who the rest of the crew is?"

"Sure," I said, wandering back to check out the poster.

"Do you know Harsha Chowdury?" Latisha asked.

I immediately pictured Harsha's straight, glossy, chin-length black hair, his dark eyes, and brilliantly white smile. "Hello? Is there a female in Hopetown who doesn't?"

"I think he's going to coordinate the stage crew."

"Ohwow. Good plan, Latisha. Very good plan," I said.

"And Hunter from KCH is going to coach vocals and run sound," she continued.

I smiled. "He's gorgeous. And great with sound."

Lamont glanced up from painting to say, "Thanks."

I rolled my eyes. "Not you, Lamont. You don't go to James Moore."

Latisha said, "And Makayla Simmons is going to coordinate choreography."

I didn't try to hide my surprise. "Makayla Simmons? What are you thinking, Latisha?"

"I'm thinking it's an *all school* talent show," she answered. "I want everyone involved. Makayla brings a whole different crowd with her."

"That's the truth." I sat down on the grass. "Listen, Latisha, I'm sorry, but I think my first act as talent show coordinator is to veto your Makayla plan."

"Did I say you could pick your title?" Latisha asked. "Let me take that back. You are not the talent show coordinator, Trin. I am the director, so we don't need a coordinator. What I need is an assistant. And the assistant director does not have veto powers. The assistant just assists. So do you want to do that, or not?"

I closed my eyes.

Work with Makayla? Ew.

But I had to get my hands on this talent show.

"Of course, Latisha," I answered. "I'm way happy to be assistant director."

•••

Monday

"So, any thoughts on publicity?" Latisha asked when math ended on Monday.

"You'll be amazed," I promised, gathering up my books. "But can I wait to tell you? I want you to be surprised with everyone else."

"Well, I—" she began as she followed me out the door.

"Hey, isn't that Chaz Keppler?" I interrupted, nodding toward a short guy with wavy hair digging in his locker. "Isn't he interclub president?"

"Yeah," Latisha answered, looking his direction with a sneer. "He's the one who nominated me for talent show director."

"Then you need to write him a thank-you note," I told her. I looked down at my outfit — perfect. I had spent extra time getting ready this morning, and now I was glad. I pushed my way through the stream of students until I reached Chaz and waited for him to look at me.

I flashed my biggest smile. "Chaz, I'm Trin Adams," I began. "I'm Latisha's assistant director for this year's talent show."

He laughed as he slammed his locker shut. "How'd she rope you into that?"

I stood up straighter. "I volunteered. I'm going to revolutionize the show."

He stopped smiling. "You're crazy. It can't be done."

"I think it's pitiful that a school as fabulous as James Moore has such a lame show," I explained. "How does it happen, when people as talented as you hold leadership positions?"

He put his hands up. "Wait a minute. I don't have anything to do with the talent show."

"Yes, you do," I contradicted. "Student council is in charge of the show, and you're probably the most important person on student council."

He grinned. "How do you figure that?"

"As interclub president, you're over every club on campus. You have connections, Chaz. And serious power."

He puffed his chest out and ran a hand through his wavy hair.

I whipped out my PDA. "I really need to schedule a time to talk to all the club presidents. I want to let them know this year's show is going to be amazing." I looked up at him. "Don't you have an interclub meeting tomorrow?"

"Yeah. During lunch in room 212. Why don't you come?"

"I'd love to."

He lowered his voice. "Look, I can't promise what kind of reaction you'll get. The talent show has always been kind of a joke, you know?"

I said, "Believe me, I know."

• • •

After school, Mello and I hopped into the car with Harmony and her sister Julia.

"Thanks for driving us around, Julia," I said. "This is going to be way cool."

She smiled. "No *problema*. Where to?"

"First stop, Cooper's Copies," I answered.

At the copy shop I asked Harmony and Mello to each pick three colors of paper. I handed them an entire ream—500 sheets—of each color, and we walked up to the counter.

"I need copies of this flyer," I told the guy behind the counter. I stacked the six packages of paper in front of him.

"If you want all different colors, you need to choose from over there," he said, pointing to a shelf of rainbow-hued sheets.

"But I'd like a whole ream of each color," I explained.

He raised his eyebrows. "You want *three thousand* copies?"

"Yes, please."

"OK, then, I'll get started," he said with a sigh.

"Trin!" Mello whispered. "Three thousand copies? Have you lost your mind?"

Harmony joined in. "We don't even have three thousand students at James Moore."

I pulled them close and squealed. "Picture this: The bell rings tomorrow. The doors open and everyone heads inside, expecting another boring day at school. But they step in and—ohwow!—everywhere they look, they see these flyers. On every locker, every classroom door, every drinking fountain. A total explosion of color that can't be missed."

Harmony grinned. "Cool frijoles, Trin. What a great idea."

Mello crossed her arms. "Let me guess. Who's going to *put* the flyers on every locker, every door, every fountain?" she asked.

I batted my eyelashes at her. "Well, I thought you'd want to help. But I can do it alone if I have to."

Harmony threw one arm around Mello and one around me. "Of course we'll help, Trin."

Back in the car I told Julia, "Next stop, channel 34's office."

"TV?" Mello asked.

I nodded. "If I don't tell them about the show, they'll feel cheated after they hear how great it turned out."

"Trin, you don't even know what any of the acts are yet," Harmony said.

I sighed. "True, but that can't be helped. It will be too late for this kind of publicity by the time I know what the acts are. Besides, our closing act is going to rock *so* hard. Just the

Chosen Girls song will be enough to make this the best talent show in California."

I caught a what-is-she-thinking look between Mello and Harmony, but I decided to ignore it and forge ahead. I left flyers at channel 34, channel 9, and channel 72. I also hit four radio stations, who promised to run free ads for me.

This show was going to rock the world, and I didn't want *anyone* to miss it.

chapter • 4

...

Tuesday

The next morning, we knocked on the front door of the school at 6:45 a.m.

"You mean you didn't get permission to do this?" Mello asked.

Harmony put her box of copies on the cement and sat down. "We might as well get comfortable. The doors are locked, and I doubt anyone will show for at least another thirty minutes."

I heard someone singing in a rich bass voice. I put my face to the glass and saw a custodian sweeping on the far end of the main hall. I knocked harder.

The man stopped singing and walked in our direction. "See?" I asked. "Perfect timing."

He spoke through the door, without opening it. "How can I help you?"

"I'm Trin Adams, the assistant director for this year's talent show," I explained. "I have three thousand flyers about the show that have to be put up before school opens today. Could you please let us in?"

"What talent show?"

I waved a flyer in front of him. "The school talent show."

He leaned his head to one side and asked, "*This* school's talent show? You made three thousand flyers about the *James Moore* talent show?"

I turned to Mello and Harmony. "Even the custodians know how bad the show is."

Mello shrugged. Harmony said, "We've been trying to tell you, Trin."

I looked at the man again. "Please?"

He said, "I'm not sure I'm supposed to unlock the doors."

"But can you imagine how long it will take for us to put up this many flyers?" I asked. "And it would be impossible to do when the halls are full of students."

"I don't know."

I smiled at him. "Does anyone else on your crew sing as well as you do?"

He ducked his head shyly. "Sing?" he asked.

"I heard you. You have a great voice," I told him. "And I think it would be way fabulous if you could get some of the rest of the crew together and enter an act in the talent show."

"No, no. I don't wanna be in no talent show," he said, shaking his head vigorously.

"But this year's show is going to be amazing. That's what these flyers are about. If you'll unlock the door, I'll show you."

He reached in his pocket and pulled out a huge ring of jangling keys. "She wants me to sing in the show!" he mumbled as he turned a key in the lock. He pulled the door open, and we stepped inside.

I handed him a flyer and encouraged him to show up for tryouts. Then we got to work, putting a different color flyer on each locker — top and bottom. When we got to the end of the hall, we turned back to look. The effect was stunning.

We shrieked and jumped up and down. But I reminded them, "That's one hall. We've got seven to go."

"My back hurts. I'm doing top lockers next time," Mello complained.

By 7:40, every locker, door, and drinking fountain had a flyer. "We have twenty minutes and a few hundred flyers left. Any ideas?" I asked.

"We could do bathroom stalls," Harmony suggested.

"Brilliant!" I agreed. "I'll hit this one. Mello, can you get the guys' bathroom across the hall?"

"Ew! I will not!" she answered.

I looked at Harmony. She shook her head.

"Fine, then. I'll do it. Harmony, guard the door," I directed. I grabbed a stack of flyers and a roll of tape, took a deep breath, and headed in.

"How was it?" Mello asked when I came out.

"Weird!" I answered. "But I made it."

After we finished the rest of the bathrooms Harmony flipped her phone open to check the time. "We've still got five minutes and a bunch of flyers. What do you want us to do with them, Trin?"

"I have a great idea. Give them to me," I answered. "I'm going to put them up in Mr. Fowler's office."

"In the principal's office?" Mello asked, handing over her stack. "Harmony, we have to stop her. She's losing her mind."

I ignored Mello and walked straight to the main office and up to the counter.

Miss Lopez looked up from the computer. "How can I help you today?"

"Good morning, Miss Lopez," I said with a big smile. "I'm Trin Adams, and I'm assistant director for this year's talent show."

"That sounds fun," she gushed.

I looked at her curiously. "You're new here, aren't you?"

"First year," she agreed with a nod.

"Yes, well, anyway, this year's show is going to be huge. We want everyone to know about it."

"I think they will. I saw the flyers everywhere when I came in today," she said. "Excellent advertising. Was that your idea?"

I leaned my elbows on the counter. "Yes. I've got some left, and I'd like to surprise Mr. Fowler by putting some in his office. Can you let me in?"

She looked over both shoulders like we were planning a secret spy mission. "If you come right now," she whispered. "He's in a meeting with the custodial staff. Something about building security."

I gulped as I followed her to Mr. Fowler's door and waited while she unlocked it. "You've got ninety seconds," she hissed. "He'll be in by eight."

I didn't waste any time. I taped the flyers to his chair, his desk, and all four walls. As I taped my last copy to his computer monitor, I heard a soft knock. The door cracked open and Miss Lopez whispered, "Time's up."

I slipped out of the principal's office and back into the hall to meet Mello and Harmony before the bell rang. We stood there and watched the first students push the doors open and freeze, mouths hanging open.

"What happened?" one of the football players asked. "It looks like a rainbow exploded in here."

"I don't know," another student answered as the halls began to fill. "Must be something big."

A cheerleader read a flyer out loud. "Revolution: The James Moore Talent Show like you've never seen it before," she said. "Don't miss the dynamic exhibition that's already gotten the attention of local TV and radio stations. For information, contact Trin Adams."

I quickly turned and opened my locker door and practically buried my head inside so they couldn't see me. But I kept listening as they moved closer.

"Who?"

"Trin Adams. Isn't she the lead singer for the Chosen Girls?"

"Yeah, you're right. Look—it says on the flyer the Chosen Girls are doing an amazing grand finale."

"So she thinks she can move here and turn our sorry talent show into something that will make the news?"

I couldn't help giggling when the football player answered, "Looks like she already has."

During lunch I went to the interclub council meeting in room 212. After they'd read their minutes and other boring stuff, Chaz introduced me.

I looked around the room of club presidents, munching on sack lunches and checking the clock on the wall.

"Thanks for letting me come today," I began. "I feel honored to have the chance to speak to you, the leaders of our school, and I won't waste your time. Did any of you notice the flyers in the halls this morning?"

Bailey, the president of the chess club, said, "Flyers? What flyers?" and everyone laughed.

I laughed too. "This year's talent show theme is Revolution, because it isn't going to be like anything James Moore has ever had before. Do you know who's going to transform it from a school-wide joke into something we can be proud of?"

Dylan, the key club president, raised his eyebrows. "You?" he asked.

"I'd love to," I admitted. "But no, it's going to be each of you. You presidents know the people in your clubs. They look up to you, respect you—that's why they chose you to lead. I'm offering you a chance to do something big for our school. Instead of just getting through the year, let's make it a year no one will ever forget."

"Um, how?" asked Kelsey, the drill team captain.

"Make sure someone in your club or organization tries out for the talent show. Preferably someone who's, well—"

"Actually talented?" Chaz asked.

"Yes, please," I agreed. "You'll want your group represented, because if the winning act has three or more members from a club on campus, the whole club gets a pizza party!"

"Even if it's the drill team?" Kelsey asked.

I nodded.

"Wow!"

I watched as everyone processed the news. They nodded, smiled, whispered.

"That's it," I finished. "Just get out there and recruit some great acts."

They mobbed me as we poured out of room 212. I answered questions about tryouts and possible acts, but I still managed to hear other people in the hall, and in science before the bell rang. Everyone seemed to be talking about the talent show—and what a great job Trin Adams was doing coordinating it.

I couldn't wait to talk to Latisha!

I rushed to math as soon as science was over. "What do you think?" I asked the second she walked into the room. "Are you amazed?"

"The flyers are great, Trin," she answered, sliding into her seat. "I noticed you put your name as the contact person."

I felt my face flush. "Well, yeah. I just thought I'd save you the headache of answering all the dumb questions. You know, when are tryouts, where are tryouts, blah, blah, blah—"

She got out her folder. "How thoughtful of you."

"Listen, Latisha, I'm sorry. I didn't even think about it. I mean, it didn't seem like a big deal."

"It's not," she said with a sigh. "I guess I overreacted, Trin. Sorry. I'm sure you came in here expecting a 'good job' instead of a slap on the wrist."

I grinned. "Well, yeah, I thought you'd be excited. Everyone's talking about the show. People are totally psyched. And that's not all—I met with interclub today and asked all the groups on campus to—"

"Trin Adams, please come to my desk," the teacher called.

Latisha's eyebrows shot up in surprise, and I'm sure mine did the same. Did we miss the starting bell or something? I hadn't heard it.

I walked the very long path up to Mr. Roberson's desk, and he handed me a little yellow note. The top read: From the Desk of Principal Fowler. Underneath, in messy blue ink, it said: Mr. Roberson, please send Trin Adams to my office immediately.

I had forgotten about my way fabulous idea to decorate Principal Fowler's office.

"Go ahead and take your books. It may be a while," Mr. Roberson said. "Do you have a friend you can call?"

"To go with me?" I asked. My voice sounded small and afraid, even to me.

He shook his head. "To get help with today's lesson if you need it."

"Yeah, Latisha," I answered. I went to my desk for my books and made my way very slowly to the office.

When I walked in, Miss Lopez raised sad eyes to me before she punched the button on her desk. "Trin Adams here to see you, sir," she said into the intercom.

"Send her in," his voice boomed.

I swallowed the lump in my throat and opened his door. The talent show posters still covered the walls. I tried to not to look at them. "Have a seat," Mr. Fowler said, pointing to a hard plastic chair opposite his desk.

I'd never seen him up close before, but for some reason I always thought he had a sense of humor hidden beneath his serious principal exterior. Now, looking at his gray hair, dour face, and pin-striped suit, I decided I might have misjudged him.

"I met with the custodial staff this morning, Trin," he began. "My head custodian told me you asked to be let into the building before hours. Despite regulations that clearly state no student is allowed into the building early, he let you in. Is that true?"

"Yes, sir."

"And as I read these flyers, it appears that you are also the party responsible for covering the entire school — even the boys' restrooms — in rainbow-colored paper. Is that also true?"

"Yes, sir."

"And according to Miss Lopez, you requested access to my personal office when I was out. Although Miss Lopez hasn't been here long, she of course knew better than to allow a student into my office, unsupervised. And yet she unlocked the door for you. Is this true?"

I hung my head. "Yes, sir."

"Trin, I'm curious. What is it about you that causes otherwise responsible people to make very poor decisions?"

I looked up at him and said, "I'm not sure, sir."

He nodded. "Then answer this question. What on earth made you come into the principal's office and paper it?"

"I'm just so excited about the talent show, sir," I answered, scooting to the edge of my seat. "It's always been terrible, see? A real embarrassment for our school. And I don't think that's right for a school as great as James Moore. So I'm revolutionizing it this year."

"And you wanted me to know?" he asked, with the barest hint of a smile.

"More than that," I said with my own smile.

He leaned back and crossed his arms. "You want me to come," he declared. "OK, Trin, I'm intrigued. I'll come see your revolutionized talent show."

I leaned forward. "Actually, sir, I wanted to ask you to be in it."

His eyes got huge and he laughed. "Me? Do an act?"

"It could be advertised as a mystery act. No one would know until that night and then — ohwow! The students would love it!"

He put his elbows on his desk and rested his chin on his fists. "They'd be surprised, wouldn't they?"

"Oh, yeah."

"I just might do it," he said. And now I definitely saw a twinkle in his blue eyes. "Maybe a lip-synch. I bet John and Susan would do it with me."

I didn't know who John and Susan were.

"Oh, I mean Mr. Roberson and Mrs. Gates, the yearbook sponsor," he corrected.

"Ohwow, yes, please! That's way fabulous, Mr. Fowler! I'll put you on the list!" I stood up and shook his hand, anxious to get out before he changed his mind. I stepped toward the door.

"Trin," he said.

I turned back.

"I'm impressed. You keep up the good work. We've never had a director like you."

I smiled and said thanks. I was in the hall before I realized he had assumed I was the talent show director.

Oh, well, so everyone was confused about that. I didn't need to run around correcting them. They'd figure it out soon enough.

...

chapter 5

Friday

The final bell rang Friday, and I wanted to run home. Instead, I held my head high as I started down the hall that led to the auditorium. Talent show tryouts would start in fifteen minutes.

I didn't even see Harmony and Mello until I almost ran into them. "Are you sure you don't want us to come?" Harmony asked. "We'd make good judges."

Mello giggled. "But it may be hard to choose. Didn't Sammy sign up for blowing bubbles with chewing gum? I heard he can blow one the size of a softball. And then Jatira says she can keep two hula hoops going at the same time — around her neck."

"Very funny," I mumbled, speaking softly enough that the students rushing by on either side of us couldn't hear me. "So no one good signed up. The show is going to be a huge flop, and my name is all over it. Trin Adams is going to be a school joke. Forever." I sniffed a couple times and looked away. "I realize how badly I've ruined my life without you rubbing it in, Mello." I pushed past them and stomped down the hall.

Harmony caught up with me and matched me stride for stride. "Look, Trin, it's not your fault. You did everything you could to get people to sign up. Posters, TV, radio, the pizza party contest—all way smart ideas."

"I didn't mean to hurt your feelings," Mello added as she joined us. "Harmony's right—it's not your fault. You didn't understand what you were up against. You're talented and beautiful and smart and fun, Trin. But even you can't expect to come in and turn our famously lame show into a raging success overnight."

I ignored Mello and pushed open the door to the auditorium.

"We tried to tell you that," she continued. "Why didn't you listen to—"

My heart beat in double time as I looked over the auditorium. I had expected it to be mostly empty. Instead, students sat, stood, wandered, talked, laughed, and sang in every square foot of the place. Basketball players, volleyball players, pep-squad members—everyone.

I spotted Latisha standing in front of the stage. "Trin, you're here!" she yelled. "Good. We've got to get started. We have forty-two acts to judge."

I turned to Harmony and Mello and said, "Looks like I'll be busy for a while."

"But, but, how—" Mello stammered. "I mean, where? Where did they come from? There were only, like, five acts signed up this morning."

"Classic James Moore," Harmony answered. "No one wanted to be the only cool act to try out. So all week they've worked the system. 'I'll do it if you do it.' Ta-dah! Forty-two acts on the last afternoon of sign-ups."

Mello grinned at me. "I was wrong, Trin, when I said you couldn't do this. I'll never doubt you again. You can do anything!"

I patted her on the shoulder and said, "That's what I like to hear." Then I started for the stage.

Someone called, "Hey, Trin. You made it happen. Good job with the show."

I smiled in that general direction and tried to figure out who said it. I spotted that football player from the hall just as he said, "Give it up for Trin Adams!" and started to clap loud, slow beats. The kids around him joined in, and soon the whole auditorium resounded with the sound of maybe a hundred students pounding their hands together and chanting, "Trin, Trin, Trin."

I felt the heat creeping up my neck, but I couldn't stop the huge smile spreading across my face. It was better than I had hoped! My plan had worked. Now everyone knew the real Trin Adams. The girl who, as Mello said, could do anything.

I hoped phase two of my plan worked just as well—getting my real father to come see the show. He probably wouldn't chant my name, but maybe he would hug me and say something like, "I never realized what I've been missing. I won't let you go again, Trin."

"Trin?"

I blinked.

Latisha got in my face. Her black eyes flashed as she said, "I'm sure it's a pretty big head trip hearing the whole student body chant your name, girlfriend, but join us here on earth for a minute. Can you calm your fans so we can get started?"

I tried to laugh. "Sure," I told her. I took the stage steps two at a time, walked to the center of the huge wooden floor, and held my hands up. As soon as the students got quiet, I said, "Thanks, everybody. But all I've done so far is hang up some posters. That and encourage you to believe in yourselves the way I believe in you. We have a great school full of talented people. This is our chance to show that to the world."

A few people cheered, and some of them clapped.

"Today is when the real work begins," I continued. "We have over forty acts trying out, and only fifteen spots. Not all of you will make the cut, but don't be discouraged. Just by trying out, you're showing what you're made of. You're brave enough to make a change. Brave enough to go against the flow. That makes you part of the best talent show our school has ever had. You're all part of the revolution!"

The whole place erupted into cheers and applause. I beckoned for Latisha to join me onstage.

"I said to calm them down," she complained when she reached me.

I grinned at her.

When the cheering died off I said, "Latisha here is going to run our tryouts today. Listen to her and have your act ready when she calls your name."

She said, "First up, Jose Martinez and his dog, Fluffball."

I left the stage and saw that a piece of paper with my name on it marked my seat on the front row.

Right next to Harsha. And Makayla.

I smiled at Harsha as I picked up my score sheets and sat down.

"I think I'm in the wrong place," Makayla griped. "I thought I came to judge the talent show tryouts, but this sounds more like a political rally."

I ignored her and pointed to the stage. "Oh, look," I said, "Fluffball is going to jump through a hoop. What a cute dog!"

I wrote *Cute Dog* on Jose's score sheet.

"Fluffball is the perfect name for her," Harsha agreed. "I don't think I've ever seen so much hair on such a little — hey, is Jose lighting that hoop?"

I covered my mouth as the large ring burst into flames.

"Can he do that?" Hunter asked, leaning forward from his seat on the other side of Makayla. "Won't we get in trouble for cruelty to animals or something?"

"We've got to save Fluffball!" I cried, ready to jump out of my seat. But Fluffball decided to save himself. He scampered off the stage and started down the aisle. Then he ducked into one of the rows and everyone climbed on their seats and screamed like he was a raving wolf instead of a six-pound Pomeranian. When Jose finally caught his dog, Latisha gently suggested he might rethink his act and come back at the end of tryouts. Then she looked at her list. "Our second act is Belinda Carino on her pogo stick," she announced.

Harsha shook his head as he wrote Belinda's name on the next sheet. "This is the kind of act that made the show famous in the past."

Hunter leaned up again and said, "Do something, Trin. Everyone's going to walk out and you're going to be left with flaming Fluffball and bouncing Belinda."

Makayla huffed, "Hunter, Harsha, aren't you supposed to be running sound and moving stuff around onstage or something?"

Harsha smiled that brilliant smile that makes my heart skip a beat. "During the show, yes. But for today, Latisha found someone else to cover so we could help judge."

"Well, then. Hunter, would you like to trade seats with me?" she asked in her snottiest voice. "That way you won't have to continue to lean over me as if I'm not here."

He stood up and said, "Sure."

I said, "Thanks, Makayla," as she rolled her eyes and moved over.

"Hunter's right," Harsha agreed as the old song "Jump!" filled the room. Belinda's ringlets extended and compressed like golden slinky toys as she bounded across the stage. "Latisha's going to kill the show if she lets the first five acts to sign up try out back to back."

I scooted to the edge of my seat, and as soon as Belinda's song ended I ran to Latisha. "Give me the list," I demanded.

"But I need to announce the next—"

"Give it to me now," I said, holding out my hand.

She gave it to me.

I scanned it quickly, looking for the most popular people in school. I found the drill team captain and her buddies half-way down. "We're going to mix it up a little," I announced. "Next up, Kelsey Carter and friends."

They squealed and fussed and took about five minutes getting to the stage.

"What are you doing?" Latisha asked, grabbing her paper. "You don't think I can read names from a list?"

"Just trust me," I answered. "Don't do all the losers at once. Get some cool people onstage, so everyone sees the potential." I patted her on the back. "You're doing a great job, director."

Kelsey and her buddies did an awesome dance routine. Their music rocked, and at one point the stage lights switched to black lights that made their costumes glow. The audience went crazy.

Harsha and Hunter high-fived me, and I knew we were on our way to an amazing show. But then Latisha called up Bentley Tarnum.

"Here we go again," Harsha said.

Hunter whispered, "Poor Bentley. He's a nice guy, really."

"What's wrong with him?" I asked.

"You'll see," Harsha answered.

I cringed as the tallest, skinniest guy I had ever seen started up the steps with a portable keyboard under one long arm ... and tripped. The keyboard hit the stage, hard, and skidded about ten feet across the smooth floor before it came to a stop. Bentley scrambled after the instrument, tripping once more before he reached it. In the process he lost his glasses. He knelt on the ground feeling around for them until Latisha stepped forward, found them, and handed them to him.

Makayla and most of the other students laughed, but I wanted to cry.

Latisha stayed with Bentley and helped him get set up. The lights went down and colored spotlights flashed on a rising cloud of fog.

"That actually looks really cool," I whispered, but I could hear people behind me snickering. I understood why—cool lights and fog just didn't fit with the guy we'd just seen sprawled across the stage.

Bentley started to play. He got maybe eight measures into the song when my heart began to beat in time with his keyboard. He totally rocked! I clapped on the backbeats because I couldn't help myself. Soon everyone joined in, and I looked behind me. I saw my feelings reflected in their faces: total shock, but also real joy, at finding something wonderful in such an unexpected place.

I couldn't tell if Bentley even realized what was happening. He was somewhere else — totally lost in his music. I wanted to shake him and say, "Look! Don't miss this! They love you."

When he struck the final rich chord, he opened his eyes and looked out at us. The cheer that greeted him was even louder than the music. I stood and clapped and screamed.

Bentley didn't move. He just stayed there, blinking, as the lights came on. Then, slowly, a grin spread over his face. He picked up his keyboard and (without tripping) left the stage.

When tryouts ended, Latisha sent everyone but our crew home. She smiled at us. "What do you think?"

"It's going to be hard to narrow it down," Harsha said.

Hunter flipped through his judge sheets. "I have so many high scores—"

"It worked!" I squealed, jumping up and down with joy. "This is *so* going to be the best show ever."

"Please," Makayla said. "It's not like we're hosting the finals for *American Idol*. I'll admit the acts were better than last year, but—"

Latisha laughed. "Better than last year? Makayla, you're part of our crew. Go ahead and let loose. Celebrate with us."

Makayla shrugged. "Whatever. Let's just start narrowing it down so we can go home."

It took us thirty minutes to agree on the top fifteen acts. I made sure they added a "mystery act" (Principal Fowler) and the bonus grand finale (The Chosen Girls). Latisha looked over the final list, which included Bentley on keyboard and Kelsey's dance routine. "OK, I'll post this on the main bulletin board, and people can check it Monday morning," she said.

"Really?" I asked.

She let out a long breath and glared at me. "I take it my assistant director has another suggestion."

"It just doesn't seem terribly dramatic," I said with a shrug.

"It's the way we've always announced who made the show," she explained.

I said, "No offense, but is that what you want? To do things the way they've always been done?" I paused to look at Makayla and the guys. "I mean, I thought we wanted a revolution."

"Yeah," Hunter agreed. "Revolution."

"She's right," Harsha added.

Makayla rolled her eyes at the guys. "So what's your idea?" she asked me.

I thought for a minute. "Let's put a sign on the bulletin board like always, but this one says tryouts were great and the results will be announced during last period or something. That way everyone will be nervous all day — and hearing it at the same time like that will be way cool."

"Sounds good," Latisha agreed.

Makayla stood up and practically threw her judge sheets at Latisha. "That's it. Take my name off the list. Find someone else for choreography." As she started up the aisle she muttered, "This isn't the James Moore talent show. It's the Trin Adams show."

Latisha stood up and called, "Makayla!"

"Let her go," I said. "She's had an attitude problem from the beginning. Please! The Trin Adams show. Where'd she come up with that?"

Latisha sighed. "Harsha, Hunter, why don't you guys go on home? Thanks for all your help. Trin and I will finish up."

The guys left, and I hopped up to collect all the judging sheets.

Latisha said, "Trin, sit down."

"But I'm just gonna—"

"Sit down."

I sat.

"Makayla is right," Latisha began.

"Makayla is jealous," I complained.

Latisha stood over me and crossed her arms. "She's the person I chose to coordinate choreography. You will apologize to her and invite her back onto the crew."

"What?"

"I want her to be part of this show," Latisha insisted. "Just like I want you to be part of the show. Do you hear what I'm saying? A *part*. Not the whole thing."

My face felt hot. "Aren't you the one who whined about *having* to be in charge of the talent show? I think you called it social suicide. Instead, I handed you the whole student body, pumped up and cheering."

"They were chanting *your* name."

I shifted uncomfortably in my seat. "Look, Latisha, I've done everything I can to make you look good. I'm sorry you aren't pleased with the results."

"I am pleased. It's just—" she sighed. "Try to remember *I'm* the director. OK?"

I smiled at her, glad the lecture was over. "Absolutely! I'll remember, Latisha," I agreed, standing to go. "Hey, give me that list of acts, and I'll take it to Principal Fowler, OK? I think he'll love my idea of announcing the winners."

chapter • 6

• • •

Saturday

"We rocked!" Harmony said as we left the tryout room at Pizza Pete's Saturday morning. "We have *so* got this contract wrapped up."

"Why do I feel like I'm in the middle of an instant replay?" Makayla asked, stepping into the hall. "Oh, maybe it's because I heard you big mouths bragging about your tryout the last time we were here."

"It's not just hot air. They sounded excellent," Lamont responded.

I added, "We're one of only two bands to get invited back."

Makayla made her eyes and her mouth into big, round circles. "Wow! Congratulations! I wonder who the other band could be." She looked around. "Oh, it must be the Makayla Simmons band. I don't see anyone else here this morning."

I wanted to growl. Instead I said, "Great. I'm glad you're here, because I need to talk to you about the whole talent show thing."

"You'll have to wait," she snapped. "I've got a tryout right now." She barked some orders to her band members, and they filed past us.

Mello looked at me, a question in her eyes. "What do you have to talk to *her* about?"

"Nothing major. But I guess I'll stick around," I answered. I didn't want them to overhear my apology so I said, "Would you take my electric, Harmony? I'll meet up with you at Java Joint."

Harmony grabbed my guitar. "We could wait."

I shook my head. "No, go on. Order me a Tuscan chicken sandwich, OK?"

I stood in the hall and tried to act like I wasn't listening to Makayla's band. They sounded really good, but we were better.

I hoped.

I forced myself away from the tryout room and wandered down the hall. As I passed an open office door, I heard a conversation that made me stop in my tracks.

"Hey, Manuel," a woman said. "Have you ordered the costumes for the new ad campaign? The boss wants to start shooting this week."

"I know," a man answered. "But they haven't chosen the band yet. I figured I'd wait until they decided, so I can get the right sizes. The costume company promised they could overnight them."

My hand flew to my heart. Costumes? Not an option. Our most embarrassing moment as a band had involved three chicken costumes, and I did not want to top that by showing up on TV wearing large slices of pepperoni pizza.

Not when everything else was going so well.

But for Makayla, on the other hand, I kind of liked the thought of seeing her in a goofy suit of some sort. Maybe it wouldn't be a pizza slice. Maybe Makayla would be a big tomato, and Jamie would be a mushroom. The new girl, Reesie, could be a container of parmesan cheese. Poor Reesie. She seemed so nice. I felt bad for her, but she should have chosen better friends.

I waited a minute more, and then I knew what I had to do. My pride—and the pride of our whole band—was at stake.

I burst through the office door and said, "Excuse me?"

"Can I help you?" the man behind the desk asked.

"Well, I happened to hear you mention the costumes, and how you're in a hurry. I wanted to tell you to go ahead and order them. For the Makayla Simmons band. The Chosen Girls are withdrawing."

"And you are—"

"Sorry. I'm Trin Adams, lead singer for the Chosen Girls."

He raised his eyebrows. "And you want to pull out of the contest?"

"Yes, please," I answered. "We have a . . . conflict of interest."

He said, "OK, then, I'll tell the boss he's got his band and we'll move ahead."

I let out a huge sigh of relief. "Thanks. Thanks so much."

I practically floated out of his office and back down the hall just as Makayla's band came out of the tryout room.

"You better be nervous," she called. "We were all over it in there."

It occurred to me that Makayla would think they beat us. I couldn't stand the snotty comments she would make about that, so I said, "The Chosen Girls decided to withdraw."

She smirked. "Yeah, right."

"I'm beyond serious," I insisted. "I just went to the office and told them. The regional ad campaign is all yours."

She and her band members looked at each other in shock. "Their tryout must have been *so* bad," she told them. "Wow. They must have really muffed it."

"No, we rocked. Big-time," I said.

"Yeah. And then you withdrew, because you wanted my band to get the money and the regional television exposure." She snorted. "Why do I not believe that?"

I held my head high. "Believe whatever you want, but I have no doubt we would have won. We chose to withdraw and that's the truth."

"Why?"

I swallowed. "I'm not going to tell you why."

Makayla tucked a strand of her silvery-blonde hair behind her ear and said, "I think I know. You losers finally figured out who has the better band. Congrats on facing up to the hard, cold facts."

I had to picture her in a big, round, bright red tomato suit to keep from telling her the real reason we dropped out.

"Now what did you hang around for?" Makayla asked. "If you're hoping to talk me into coming back to the talent show, forget it."

"That's up to you," I said. "I just needed to apologize for—" What could I say? *I'm sorry I have so many great ideas. I'm sorry Hunter and Harsha like me better than you.* "I'm sorry I got on your nerves yesterday," I finished.

She squinted her steel-grey eyes at me. "You handed us the ad campaign, and now you're apologizing to me?"

I nodded.

"Hmm. Well, tell Latisha I'll *think* about coming back," she said.

"I'll tell her," I said. "And now I'm outie. I'm meeting my buds at Java Joint."

•••

Harmony slammed her glass onto the table so hard some of her frozen cappuccino shot into the air. "You *what?*" she blared.

"I pulled us out of the ad contest," I repeated. "But give me a chance to tell you why. I promise you'll thank me."

Mello said, "This better be good."

Lamont took a huge bite of his burger and murmured, "Mm-hm."

"They wanted us to do the ads in costume!" I explained. "It would have been the Chik'n Quik nightmare all over again, but on TV. Being played day after day, in four states!"

Mello tilted her head. "I don't get it. Why would Pizza Pete's want us to wear chicken costumes for a pizza commercial?"

"Not chicken costumes," I said, rolling my eyes. "Big pieces of pizza or tomato suits or something."

"You didn't bother to find out what the costumes look like, exactly?" Lamont asked.

I threw my hands up. "Does it matter? I refuse to be seen on television dressed as any form of vegetable or junk food." I looked at Harmony and Mello. "I assumed you would feel the same way. Who cares about the money we'd make if we have to be publicly humiliated?"

"I still think you could have checked with us," Harmony said. "We should make decisions like that as a band. Together."

Mello said, "Yeah. How hard would it be to call?"

"You're right," I admitted. "I'm sorry." I took a bite of my sandwich.

Harmony started to giggle. "I take it Makayla doesn't know about the costumes?"

I shook my head and grinned while I chewed.

The bells over the Java Joint door jangled.

"Speak of the—" Lamont said.

Makayla came in with a shopping bag in one hand and a satchel in the other. "Chosen Girls!" she called. "I'm so glad you're still here." She marched right back to our booth and announced, "I bought each of you a little something."

"Ohwow!" I said, thinking my apology must have really made an impact on her.

"How sweet of you, Makayla." I held my hands out, anxious to see what she had gotten.

She pulled a neon green T-shirt out of the bag and put it in my hands. In huge, bold blue letters the logo printed on the front read, The Makayla Simmons band ROCKS!

She handed one to Mello and one to Harmony. "I thought green seemed like an appropriate color. You know, since you're all green with envy. Now, don't forget to wear them to school *every* day. Won't it be fun? And just think of all the time you'll save choosing outfits this week!"

"No way," Harmony said, trying to hand hers back. "We said whoever *won* the contest had to wear the other band's shirts. Your band didn't really win. You only got it because we dropped out."

Makayla didn't take the shirt. "How quickly you forget. Or pretend to forget. Actually, our agreement was only based on whoever got the contract." She reached into the satchel, pulled out a thick stack of papers, and waved it under our noses. "And that would be the Makayla Simmons band. I just happen to have the contract right here — signed, sealed, and delivered."

I leaned toward Lamont and whispered, "Save us, please."

He shook his head. "This is your deal, Trin," he whispered back. "And she's right about the agreement. They won the bet, fair and square."

Makayla put the contract away. "It didn't seem right that I should have to pay for *your* shirts, especially since I had to pay extra for the rush order. But with all the money we're getting from Pizza Pete's I decided it's no big deal."

She smiled her tight little smile that doesn't show any teeth. "So consider them my gift to you. I'll just take it out of our band's advertising budget, because you really will be giving my band some good exposure at James Moore." She waved a perky little salute, said, "See you Monday!" and left.

Harmony and Mello glared at me.

I wadded the Makayla shirt into an angry little ball. "I forgot, OK? I forgot we made that deal."

Mello held her green shirt in front of my face. "Maybe that's because *we did not* make this deal," she corrected. "*You* made this deal. You were so sure of yourself that you had to show off and now ..." She paused and took a few deep breaths. "Do you have any idea how gross I look in neon green?"

"You messed up, Trin," Harmony said. "I'd rather be dressed like a roll of Italian sausage on nationwide TV than wear this thing to school for five minutes."

I nodded in agreement. "It's going to be a very long week."

• • •

At home, I hid the Makayla shirt on the bottom of my T-shirt drawer. At least I didn't have to worry about the ugly thing until Monday.

I flopped onto my bed and started humming a tune. Then words came into my mind like a flood, and I jumped up to grab a pen and paper. I began to write:

Just when you've got the world inside your hand,
That's when nothing goes the way you planned.
You try and cry but still can't understand.
I'm gonna be stronger than the things I fight.
I'm gonna be stronger than the wrongs I right—

Of course, I thought to myself. *So the pizza thing didn't work out. I'm not going to let it get me down. I'll concentrate on the talent show instead.*

That part of my life was going well. So well, in fact, that I decided I needed to send an email to Jake.

I wrote:

> Dear Jake,
> Thanks for the text message you sent last week. I'm glad you're doing okay. I wasn't sure, since I hadn't heard from you in a long, long time.
> You said you hoped to come see me in a couple weeks. It's actually a perfect time to visit, because next weekend is the talent show at my school. The band I'm in (Chosen Girls) is doing a huge closing number with a big set and special effects

and everything. I'd love for you to see us perform.
Besides, I'm pretty much running the whole show. It's always
been really bad, so they asked me to help this year. Tryouts
were amazing, and the show's so big, it's being advertised on
the radio and will probably get covered on the news.
If you think you can come, I'll save you a special seat in the
front row.

See you soon,
Trin

chapter • 7

...

Monday

Monday morning, as soon as people saw that the winners weren't posted, they went crazy. Everyone talked about the talent show all day, and the halls were buzzing.

"Do you think you made it?"

"I don't know."

"There were *so many* good acts!"

"I don't see how we can wait all day to find out."

"We've already stressed about it all weekend."

So I'd been right — waiting definitely created suspense, which was way fun. Of course they all tried to get information out of me, but I was too strong for them. I kept my lips sealed.

Makayla kept hers sealed too — at least about the results from tryouts. I wish she'd kept them sealed, period. She visited our table during lunch and squealed, "I love your shirts! I've never seen you three looking better."

I tried to smile. "Thanks, Makayla. Believe me; we've gotten a lot of comments on them today."

"Oh? I wish I could have heard those conversations," she answered. "Did you tell people you're a big Makayla Simmons fan? Or did you unload the whole story about how my band got the contract you wanted, and they'll be seeing me on TV soon?"

"Oh, we told them to be watching for your commercial," Harmony assured her with a little smirk. "We can't wait to see it ourselves."

Makayla slid into the seat next to mine. "Listen, Latisha called yesterday in an *absolute panic*. She's *desperate* for my input on the talent show. I explained about the new contract and the stress I'm under while we're taping such a big commercial, but she just begged me."

I hated how Makayla could make it sound like she was revealing some big secret, even when talking loud enough that people three tables away could hear.

"Then this morning I ran into Hunter before school, and he said he hoped I'd keep helping with the show. And in first period Harsha told me how much he wants me to stick around," she continued. "I hardly see how I'll fit it into my schedule, but I hate to let the guys down."

"So you're back on the show?" I asked.

She stood up. "Yes, I'm back. So I guess I'll be spending my after-school hours with you the next few days, Trin. Today's the first big practice, right? And it will be even more fun since you're wearing my band's shirt."

"Ohwow, sure," I agreed. "Loads of fun."

•••

When Principal Fowler's voice finally came over the inter-com during last period, I couldn't help smiling at my class-mates. No one moved. No one made a sound. Bentley's in that class, and I especially tried to watch him without being obvious.

Principal Fowler really played the announcement up. He made a big deal out of the mystery act, and then listed everyone that made the show. I could hear the screaming break out in different classrooms down the hall as each act was announced.

After the first ten, Bentley got out a spiral notebook and started doodling like he wasn't even listening. But when the principal called his name I saw a big grin spread over his face. The whole class cheered, and he finally looked up and said, "Thanks."

Principal Fowler said, "Those of you who made the show, please head directly to the auditorium for rehearsal. And congratulations!" The bell rang, and everyone went crazy-wild talking about who made it and who didn't. I smiled as I pushed past them, anxious to get to practice.

I shouldn't have been in a hurry. Makayla was prancing all over the place and giving orders. "Josephina, your voice is amazing," she said as she walked right out onto the middle of the stage and into the middle of the first act. "But I've seen more movement in a still-life painting. If you want your act to pop, you're going to have to move. Try raising one arm like this as you sing that line about the future." She grabbed Josephina's arm and pulled it up slowly. "And during the musical interlude, don't be a such a statue. Try this." Makayla did a few side steps and a twirl.

I had to hold my hand over my mouth to keep from laughing out loud. Makayla obviously knew nothing about dance. While she worked with Josephina, I made my way back to Hunter at the sound booth.

"Makayla's doing great, don't you think?" he asked. "Josephina's act is going to be a hundred times better."

"What?" I blurted in surprise. "She doesn't know what she's doing, and she's turning Josephina's act into a joke. Look at that!" I pointed at the stage, where Josephina tried to twirl and almost lost her balance.

Hunter said, "Give her a little time, Trin. She's only been working on it for five minutes."

"Well, it would help if she had a choreographer who knew something about choreography," I huffed before I walked away. I wandered over to Harsha, who stood in the wings waiting to move props.

"It's amazing to see Makayla help someone like Josephina, isn't it?" he asked in a soft voice. "I think that's the coolest thing about this show — watching people who usually ignore each other come together. It's a revolution in more ways than one, you know?"

I stuffed my hands into the pockets of my jeans. "I guess," I answered. "But she could be nicer about it. The whole 'I've seen more movement in a painting' speech — was that necessary?"

He laughed. "Well, yeah, she *is* still Makayla. But I'm glad she's back on the crew. This is good for her."

I rolled my eyes and went back to my seat.

It almost caused me physical pain to watch Makayla work. She even told the drama-club people where to stand and how to walk during their five-minute sketch.

I couldn't think of anything to do. Latisha had no problems getting people on and off the stage, and Makayla seemed to take over on everything else. I sat there, bored, in my hideous green shirt.

But five acts later, Makayla tried to give Kelsey's group some pointers. Kelsey, the drill team captain. I couldn't take it anymore.

"Makayla, what are you doing?" I yelled, running up onstage. "Do you really think Kelsey needs your help?"

"I'm giving my opinion as choreography coordinator," Makayla answered. "The move I'm talking about looks out of place. It doesn't fit the style of the music."

I shook my head in disbelief. "Kelsey, how long have you been on drill team?" I asked, stepping past Makayla.

She said, "Three years."

"And how long have you taken dance?" I continued.

"I don't know—ten years, maybe?"

I nodded. "I thought so. Makayla, how many years of dance have you taken?"

"I took, um, a few years—a couple," she stammered.

"I'm guessing that was a while back. Like when you were five, maybe," I scoffed. "I've taken dance nonstop since I turned three. Ballet, jazz, tap, hip-hop, you name it. And I know enough to know it's flat out wrong for *you* to try to give Kelsey pointers. Besides, anyone who knows dance would say if you're going to change the move, it should look more like this." I said, giving a demonstration I thought showed off my abilities pretty well.

"Now *you're* telling me how to do my routine?" Kelsey asked.

I held my hands out and tried to look humble. "If you want some ideas, I'd be happy to help you out. I thought you might like to know *someone* on the crew has some real background in choreography."

"Actually, what Makayla said made sense," Kelsey volunteered. "That move has always bothered me."

"But you don't have to do what Makayla—"

Makayla stepped between us. "I am the director of choreo—"

"Trin," Latisha called from the wings. "Get off the stage."

I shook my head. "Trust me on this, Latisha. I know what I'm talking—"

"Then why is Kelsey agreeing with *me*?" Makayla asked.

Latisha came out and grabbed me by the elbow. She dragged me back to the side of the stage. "I need you to let Makayla do her job," she whispered. "And speaking of jobs, aren't you the director of publicity?"

"Yeah," I answered. "The whole rainbow explosion last week—remember? I did that."

"Right. Thanks for reminding me. I got your receipt for the copy bill. Three hundred and sixty dollars! Trin, that's more than our entire budget for the show," she complained.

"But it was important that—"

"And I've heard a rumor that you promised the drill team a pizza party," she interrupted. "Is that true?"

"Not necessarily the drill team. The pizza party is for whatever club has the winning act," I explained.

"Trin! The drill team has thirty members. Giving them a pizza party will cost us at least a hundred dollars."

"Are you saying you think Kelsey's act will win?" I asked, turning to watch Makayla and Kelsey work out a few more steps. "Oh! Now I see why you want Makayla to help with choreography," I exclaimed, dropping my voice to a whisper. "If Makayla messes up the drill team's act, we won't have to buy them pizza. Good thinking, but it's not really fair."

"Trin! That is *not* my plan," she countered.

"That's right. Don't admit it to anyone. It could cause a *huge* scandal," I said with a nod. "So you're probably hoping Marvin, Jacob, and Gandy win. They're in the biology club, and it has only seven members. That would take, what? Two pizzas?"

Latisha started making a weird noise. I thought it sounded something like a bear might sound right before it attacks. I took a step away from her.

She stopped growling and clenched her fists. Then she loosened her hands and let out a long breath. "Just stop spending money, OK?"

Why couldn't she understand? "If I didn't spend that money, no one would have tried out. The show would reek, like always."

"This is getting me nowhere. Let me change tacks," Latisha said. "I'll admit you did a great job advertising tryouts. But what about the show? It's this Friday night, Trin, and I haven't seen a single poster about it."

"I've got it under control," I promised. "I've got big plans. You'll be blown away."

Latisha's eyes stayed locked on mine. "How much money will it take to pull off these big plans?"

"Not much. And don't worry about the finances. Really. Ticket sales are going to bring in more than enough," I promised.

"I hope you're right," she said. "And for now, I think this is a perfect time for you to work on publicity. You do your job, and let other people do theirs."

"Fine," I answered. "I'll go work on my awesome ideas."

"And use tomorrow's rehearsal time to work on posters too."

"You mean you don't want me to help with practice— ever?" I asked, blinking in surprise.

"We'll manage without you," she said, pulling a key out of her pocket. "Here. Take my key to the stu-co office. You can work in there. And use all the supplies you want, because they're already paid for."

I wrapped my hand around the key and started for the steps. Then I turned back and said, "OK. Run rehearsals without me. But don't forget, Latisha, that if it weren't for me you'd be headed for another blowout instead of the biggest event James Moore has ever seen."

chapter • 8

...

Tuesday

Latisha probably knew special access to her office would ease my pain about getting kicked out of practice. But best of all, the office gave Harmony, Mello, and me a place to hide away from all the comments about our wearing Makayla Simmons band T-shirts two days in a row. Wearing anything two days in a row pretty much breaks every law of fashion known to the human race—but shirts with *her* name on them? Blech!

So on Tuesday afternoon, I stood at the student council office doorway with Harmony and Mello. I fumbled for Latisha's key, trying not to drop my armload of wooden stakes, metal spikes, and rope.

Mello eyed my supplies suspiciously. "I'm not sure what kind of advertising you've got in mind," she said. "I thought we'd be making posters."

"We are," I assured her, handing her the stuff so I could open the door. "But of course they won't be ordinary, blah posters." I turned the key in the lock until I heard it click.

"I've never been in here," Harmony said as we entered the room. We could tell it was just an ordinary classroom, but the walls were lined with chairman-of-the-board-type desks with officers' names on them. Harmony stopped in front of the first desk. "Woo-hoo, this is where Chaz Keppler does his lofty work."

Mello fiddled with a collection of Happy Meal toys next to the nameplate that read, Latisha Punch, Secretary. "Wow. This is, like, serious. I didn't know student council members each get their own desk."

"Only the officers do," I corrected. "And get this, they don't even call themselves *student council*. They shorten it so it sounds like, stu-co."

Harmony laughed. "Thank you, Miss In-the-Know. So when do you plan to give interclub president Keppler the boot?"

"Chaz? He's great. Why would I try to get rid of him?"

Mello crossed her arms and leaned back against Latisha's desk. "Everyone's talking about it, Trin. In one week you've done more to get the clubs involved and excited than Chaz has done in a year."

"Oh, whatever." Afraid my face might show how much the comment pleased me, I walked to the back of the room. "It looks like the supplies are back here. Let's get started."

"Trin's ignoring us," Mello said, following me. "She doesn't want to be just interclub president. She's holding out for the big-cheese title."

Harmony blocked my path. She held her fingers up to frame my face. "How about Trin Adams, *stu-co* president? It fits. You'd do a great job running the whole school."

Mello nodded. "You'd get the votes too. With this miracle you're pulling off, the whole student body adores you."

I wanted to ask for details. *Tell me what you're hearing. What wonderful things are people saying about me?* Instead I said, "You're very sweet, but I don't want to be president. I don't even want to be on stu-co. Look, they have poster board in every color. Let's use silver."

Harmony took the pieces I handed her. "At least tell us what it feels like to be everyone's favorite person."

I laughed. "Wouldn't know. Here, cut these poster boards into strips this size," I instructed. "We're going to make Burma Shave signs." I handed out scissors and started cutting my own piece.

"See how modest you are?" Mello asked, starting on hers. "No wonder everyone loves you."

"I'm not faking about that," I insisted. "If Makayla or Latisha liked me even a little bit, I'd be helping with practice right now. Instead, they've exiled me to this office. Latisha said it's so I can work on publicity, but she just wants to get rid of me."

Harmony put her strips in a pile and grabbed another poster board. "I knew it wouldn't work with Makayla. What did she do?"

I looked down at my neon green shirt. "I can't believe I'm wearing her name. When this week is over, I'm going to burn this shirt. Then I'm going to flush the ashes down the toilet."

"That's harsh. What happened?" Mello asked.

"She bossed everyone nonstop at the last practice. You'd think she was some famous dance instructor from the way she acts," I explained.

"Not that I'm a big Makayla fan, but isn't that her job? She *is* the choreography person, right?" Mello asked.

I found a thick, black marker and wrote "Revolution" in block letters on a strip of poster board. "That's the root of the problem right there," I said, writing "Auditorium" on the next piece. "Latisha never should have chosen her. She doesn't know near as much about dance as—"

"As you do?" Mello finished.

"Well, yeah."

Harmony's scissors froze in mid-cut. "Oh, Trin, please tell me you didn't point that out."

"I might have hinted at it," I admitted.

Mello put more printed strips on the pile. "You didn't say it during practice, did you?"

I shrugged.

"In front of everyone?"

I got up and looked for tacks and a hammer.

"Trin!" Harmony said. "You embarrassed Makayla in front of everyone. No wonder she's mad. And can't you see how that makes *you* look?"

"I *do* know more about dance," I answered. "I've taken lessons since I turned—"

Mello interrupted. "Not the point. Do you really want to show off like that?"

I whacked with my hammer until the first piece of poster board felt securely fastened to a wooden stake.

"How is it showing off when it's *true*?" I asked, hammering another piece to a stake.

Mello finally said, "I give up, Trin. Just talk to me about these signs. How do they work?" She looked at my two signs, which read, "8 o'clock" and "Friday night."

"They're Burma Shave signs," I said, holding them up.

Harmony handed me the last few strips. "They aren't for the talent show?"

I spread the signs out on the floor, in order. "A long time ago a company called Burma Shave used a cool way to advertise," I explained. "Instead of having one big sign beside the road, they had a bunch of small signs. They only put a little bit of information on each one. That way, when people drove by, they would look for the next sign to get the whole message. We're going to do the same thing on every side-walk on campus." I stood back to survey my work.

The signs read: Revolution is going to rock/ Auditorium 8 o'clock/ Bring $5 on Friday night/ see a show that's out of sight!

Harmony nodded. "Cool frijoles. I like it, Trin."

"Good," I said. "Now we need to make, like, four more sets, and then we'll put them up." I pointed to a massive roll of paper that stood almost as tall as me. "But first, can you both help me? I want five twenty-five – foot-long strips of that."

"For what?" Mello asked, helping me lower the top end of the heavy roll until the whole thing lay on the floor.

I smiled at them. "Has anyone ever hung a twenty-five-foot by twenty-five-foot sign on the front of the school building?"

"Never," they answered at the same time.

I gave the paper a shove, and it began to unroll. "Good," I said. "I wanted to be the first."

•••

I had to recruit my new friend the head custodian and most his workers to help hang the giant sign. We had custodians on long extension ladders, custodians on the ground, and custodians hanging out of the third-floor windows. Once they got it up, and straight, the size of it—the amazing-ness of it—took my breath away.

When I could finally speak I called up, "Ohwow! It's way fabulous! Even better than I hoped." I turned to Mello and Harmony. "Do you only love it?"

Their eyes were huge. "Sí. Muy bien," Harmony answered. "You were right about putting silver glitter on the letters. When the sun catches it, the whole thing lights up."

"No one will miss it, that's for sure," Mello added. "I'm surprised how much of the building it covers."

I read over the sign again:

REVOLUTION
All-school Talent Show
This Friday Night, 8 p.m.
Auditorium

I hope no one misses the bottom part that says "See Trin Adams for Information," I thought. *Especially Jake. If he comes. Won't he be impressed to see my name up in lights? Well, almost in lights. I mean, it's plastered across the front of the school in shiny two-foot letters.*

I pulled out my phone and checked to see if he'd called or texted yet.

Nope. Nothing.

It might be two years before you hear from him again, I warned myself. *Don't get your hopes up.*

We worked quietly for a few minutes, fastening the base of the sign. Then Harmony said, "Hey, we talked about Makayla's deal, Trin. But you haven't told us why Latisha is giving you a hard time."

I tied one of the ropes to a metal stake we had driven into the ground. "I don't know what's up. We've always gotten along pretty well, but she's kind of turned into a Nazi since we started working on the talent show."

"Like how?" Mello asked.

I moved to the next stake. "She's got it in her head that I'm trying to steal her glory or something. Like she'd have any glory to steal if I hadn't come along. I mean, please, you remember what the talent show has always been like?"

Harmony glanced up at the sign. "So what do you think has put that idea in her head?" she asked.

"I don't know," I answered. "She's incredibly sensitive. I'm paranoid all the time that she'll misunderstand something I do."

"So you're probably pretty worried about the sign then, huh?" Mello asked.

I took a few steps back and looked up at it. "No. I think she'll love it. See where it says, 'Latisha Punch, director'? I put it on so she'd know I wasn't trying to take her job."

Harmony mumbled something I couldn't understand.

"What?" I asked.

"I said it might have been more effective if you hadn't put Latisha's name *under* yours."

Mello added, "And she might like it better if her name was bigger than yours. Or at least just as big."

I rolled my eyes. "You're both as bad as she is. I'm working hard on this show, and I'm not embarrassed for people to know it. I don't see why—" I stopped and listened. "Hey, that's my phone." I pulled it out and looked.

A text from Jake!

"Is everything OK?" Harmony asked.

I looked up and flashed a big smile. "Yeah."

"Who is it?"

"It's some information I've been waiting for—about the talent show. Listen, do you mind finishing up for me? I need to run to the restroom." I flew into the building and down the hall.

Stop hoping, I told myself. *It's probably just another lame excuse why he can't come. Again.*

I had to know, either way, so I locked myself in a stall and pulled up his message.

Trin,

Thanks for the invitation. Please save that seat for me— front and center. I want to see my girl's big show.

I'll book a hotel soon.

Jake

I let my tears fall as I hugged the small silver phone to my chest. It wasn't my dad, but it was the closest I'd been to him in a long time.

chapter • 9

...

wednesday

The next morning before first period, Chaz stopped me in the hall. "Trin, the sign for the show is huge! Did you make it?"

I felt the eyes of the students around us as they slowed down and turned to look at me. I smiled. "Yeah. You like?"

"It's awesome," he answered, following me as I walked to my locker. "I'm sorry I didn't believe you at first."

I dialed my combination. "About what?"

"That you could turn the show around. You're doing a great job, Trin. Everyone thinks so."

As I opened my locker and pulled out a book, I wondered if Chaz had heard the rumblings. Did he know people thought I'd be a better interclub president than he is? I patted his arm. "Thanks, Chaz. And don't feel bad. It's not your fault you didn't think about using the talent show to get the clubs involved and all."

He looked surprised. "Huh?"

"I mean, no one has before, right?" I looked in the tiny mirror on my locker door and pulled a strand of hair into place. "I guess I have some kind of inborn skill or some —"

A cheerleader stepped between us. "Excuse me. Trin, did you think of those cute little signs lined up along the sidewalks?"

I finished my lip gloss before I said, "Sure did!"

"I knew it had to be your idea," she bubbled. "When I saw it, I just thought, 'Now that looks like something Trin Adams would do.'"

A football player named Biff or Buff or something stopped to add, "You know that's right. This talent show is going to rock, dude!"

"It will if I can help it," I agreed. I smiled at myself in the little mirror before I shut my locker and started for class.

•••

During lunch, Kelsey actually left the drill team table to come talk to me.

"Trin, I thought you'd wanna know we finally worked out that one move. It's going to go like this," She demonstrated between the tables as she counted, "Five, six, seven, eight. Step, turn, knee, arms."

"Looks good, Kelsey. I'm glad you added that spin I suggested."

A few students clapped. One called, "Go, Kelsey! Let's see the whole routine."

I stood up. "You'll have to wait until Friday night to see the rest of it."

"Will it be worth the wait, Trin?" a guy two tables over asked.

His buddy added, "And the five bucks?"

I put my hands on my hips and answered, "If the Chosen Girls' closing song was the *only* act, it would be worth the wait and the five bucks."

"Trin! Sssshhhh," Mello hissed. "We're just doing one song. It's not that big a deal."

I sat down and lowered my voice. "It will be a big deal, because I'm making it one. We've totally rocked at practice, our backdrop is amazing, and when we add the special effects—ohwow. Don't you see? I want my d—" I caught myself. "I want my classmates to be blown away. And they will be."

Harmony said, "I hope so, Trin. You're making me a little—"

Some chick named Mitzy yelled, "Just curious, Trin. If the Chosen Girls are so incredible, why have the three of you worn Makayla Simmons band shirts all week?"

I rolled my eyes. Then I forced a huge smile. "We're trying to support our classmates," I answered. "Got a problem with that?"

Makayla appeared behind me and put her hands on my shoulders. "Isn't that sweet?" she asked. "Trin, Harmony, and Mello have become some of my biggest fans. I tried to tell them, look, if you want to wear a Makayla shirt every day, I'm all for it. But at least get some different colors, you know? Add some variety."

I so wanted to slap her. Instead, I squeezed my hands together to keep from doing anything stupid.

"But they seem to love the lime green," she continued. "So now I'm just begging them to at least *wash* them between wearings." I looked back in time to see her hold her nose and grimace.

"Now you're getting close, Makayla, to what I really think about these shirts," I mumbled, squeezing my own nose for emphasis.

She looked down her nose at me and said, "Yeah, well. Two and a half more days. See you at dress rehearsal this afternoon, Trin. If Latisha lets you come."

She pranced off.

"*Is* Latisha going to let you go to dress rehearsal?" Harmony asked.

"She has to," I answered. "We're in the show."

Mello giggled. "She might keep you locked in some secret closet until everyone else is finished."

"Sī. And let you out just in time for the grand finale," Harmony added.

I shook my head. "Not funny. I mean, the talent show is my deal, start to finish. My name is all over it. And now that I know my … my family is coming, how can she expect me to just sit back? My whole reputation is riding—"

"OK, OK," Mello interrupted. "We've got it, Trin. But we aren't the ones you have to convince."

"Right," I agreed. "I'll go talk to Latisha."

• • •

She let me go to dress rehearsal.

At first I wasn't much help. I ran around like everyone else, trying to make sure the costumes, instruments, and backdrop pieces were in place and ready for my own act. I had just laid out my white super suit when I heard Latisha's voice over the sound system: "Everyone, please find a seat in the auditorium. I have a few announcements before we begin."

Mello, Harmony, and I chose seats near the front. Latisha went through the expected reminders: "This is our last rehearsal. Pretend it's the real thing. We'll try to run straight through, but if we have to stop to fix something we will."

I whispered to Harmony, "I hope she remembers to tell everyone to be here by five o'clock Friday."

"She'll remember."

"What if she doesn't? Maybe I should run up there."

I started up from my seat just as Latisha said, "You *must* be here by five o'clock Friday."

I sat back down.

"One last thing before we start," Latisha continued. "I have some people to thank. Makayla, come up here."

Makayla ran onstage and tossed her silver-blonde hair around while Latisha said nice things about her. She called up Hunter next, and then Harsha.

Mello whispered, "I can't wait to hear what she says about you."

"She won't," I whispered back. "She's going to ignore me. Watch."

But I was wrong. "And last but not least, everybody give it up for Trin Adams," Latisha said. I made my way up onstage with everyone's applause pounding in my ears and filling up my heart. Latisha continued, "I think we all know how hard Trin has worked to make this show a success."

"She won't let us forget it, either," Makayla said in voice I'm sure reached the people on the back row.

Everyone laughed. I tried to smile like I thought it was funny too.

Then Latisha said, "OK, let's get started."

I moved up to the front row, center seat. I wanted to be close in case Latisha needed my help. And I wanted to try out the seat I had saved for Jake. I sat back and ran my hands up and down the arm rests. But I hoped his arms wouldn't rest at all. I imagined him clapping his hands off, applauding me, his daughter. His daughter, who he suddenly realized deserved his love and attention.

I lost myself in that daydream for a while. I think we'd gotten to the third act before Latisha came and tugged on my arm. "We need you backstage. Help make sure the next act is ready to go on each time."

"Sure!" I agreed. "I can do that." I grabbed a program and hunted down Bentley in the hall backstage.

"You're on next," I told him.

He nodded.

"Where's your keyboard?"

He pointed to it. It stood between an inflatable saxophone and a step ladder across the hall.

"Well, go get it!" I demanded. "We can't have any down-time. This show has to be professional."

Bentley shook his head.

I ran and peeked at the stage. Kelsey's girls had maybe two minutes left. I made my way back to Bentley.

"What's your deal?" I asked. "It's time. Are you going to get the keyboard or not?"

He said, "Harsha told me not to."

"Really?" I asked. "Well, I'm assistant director and I think you better listen to *me*. I mean, does that make sense to you? How are you going to play your keyboard if it's not on the stage? Go get it and be ready for them to call you."

He shook his head again.

"Fine," I said. "I'll get it."

The keyboard was heavier than I expected. I had a hard time getting a grip on it too, because of its awkward shape. When I finally managed to lift it from the ground, I started for the stage. "Excuse me," I called to the students milling around. "Please let me through."

Josephina asked, "Why are you carrying that?"

I rolled my eyes. "You know—if you want something done right, you've got to do it yourself."

Some brown-haired guy I'd never seen before came up beside me and said, "Here, Trin, let me take that."

"I've got it," I answered. "Do I look like a wimp or something? You don't think I can handle it?" At the edge of the stage, I put the instrument down long enough to catch my breath. Then Kelsey's dance team finished and ran in my direction.

"Excuse me," I repeated as I made my way onto the pitch-black stage. Oh wow, was it ever dark! I remembered Bentley's huge fall during tryouts and hoped I wouldn't star in the sequel. I wondered how many cords might be strung across the stage, waiting to trip me. I tried to avoid them, but when I looked down, I realized I couldn't see past the keyboard to the floor even if the lights were on.

I guessed at where center stage might be and left the keyboard there. I rushed back to Bentley and gave him a shove onto the stage.

The fog and colored lights began, and the spotlight fell on Bentley. But he just stood there, because he hadn't gone to the right spot. I could see the dim outline of his keyboard about ten feet away.

Latisha yelled, "Stop! Lights up!"

The stage lights came on and revealed a blinking Bentley about four good strides from his instrument.

"Harsha!" Latisha yelled. "What happened?"

Harsha ran onto stage. His brilliant, heart-stopping smile was nowhere to be seen. "Get out here, Wesley," he called.

That same brown-haired boy from backstage came forward.

"Show me the glow-in-the-dark *K*," Harsha demanded.

Wesley pointed to a *K* on the floor in front of Bentley.

"Show me the keyboard," Harsha continued.

Wesley pointed to the keyboard.

"Your instructions were to put the keyboard on the *K*," Harsha said. "Why did you put it over there?"

"I didn't," Wesley answered.

It looked like things could get ugly. I checked my program and decided it might be a good time to look for the next act. But I hadn't gone far when I heard Harsha's voice. "Trin! Get out here!"

I walked onstage and said, "Look, Harsha, I'm sorry. I—"

"Are you going to tell me you're better at handling the stage crew than I am?" he asked.

"No."

"That you've studied props and blocking since you turned three?"

"No."

"That you thought Bentley should know *someone* on our staff has a background in stage setup?"

I felt the heat rising on my face. "No."

"Then why did you try to take over my job?" he asked.

I couldn't stand the look in his eyes, so I turned away. But I looked right at Makayla, who wore a very satisfied smirk on her face. No doubt she recognized his whole speech as the things I had said to her about me being better at dance.

Behind her, the rest of the students in the show had stopped talking and wandering around. Everyone stood still, watching and listening.

"You're good at some stuff, Trin. But that doesn't mean you're good at everything. Let us do our own jobs," Harsha finished.

I said, "Forgive me for trying to help. I'll get out of everyone's way now." Then I went backstage and found a door that led outside.

I sat under my favorite palm tree and let the tears fall. *Why is everyone so mad at me?* I wondered. *It was an easy mistake to make. Why can't they understand that all I want is an excellent show?*

I breathed deeply and pulled myself together. Trin Adams had too much to do to sit around crying. I wiped my face and made myself smile, even though no one was around to see me. Then I thought of a couple new lines for the song I had started.

I'm gonna be stronger than the door that's slammin' in my face.

I'm gonna be stronger than the thoughts I'm needing to replace . . .

Sometimes it feels so hard just gettin' through the day,
But that's not gettin' in my way.

"Trin?"

I looked up and saw Harmony standing over me.

"It's time for our finale."

I jumped up and said, "Great! Let's rock."

She looked surprised. "Yeah, sure, OK," she agreed. "I came to see if you were all right, but you look like you're fine."

"Good," I answered, still smiling. As we waited backstage, I thought, *That's exactly what I want. I want it to look like I'm fine.*

chapter • 10

...

Thursday

At lunch Harmony said, "Let's have a bonfire after the talent show tomorrow night."

"Sounds fun!" I agreed. "Where?"

Mello put her fork down. "Are you both crazy? We're gonna be way too tired to do a bonfire. What are you thinking, Harmony?"

"She's thinking of a spectacular, fabulous way to celebrate an awesome show," I explained.

"No," Harmony corrected, tugging the neckline of her Makayla Simmons T-shirt. "Actually, I'm thinking of a spectacular, fabulous way to destroy these shirts!"

"Don't look now," Mello whispered, "but our fashion designer is headed this way."

Makayla began her speech before she got within twenty feet of our table. "Trin, Harmony, Mello!" she crooned. "Looking lovely in Makayla Simmons green! And feeling proud, I'm sure, to be connected to the band that's been chosen to do the new TV campaign for Pizza Pete's."

"You know it," I answered, hoping my sarcasm showed.

Makayla laughed her loud, irritating laugh that makes everyone stop what they're doing and look to see what's so funny. "Isn't it amusing that you're called the Chosen Girls, but you didn't get chosen? I mean, I'm thinking about how amazing this opportunity is—being on TV, making tons of money. I almost feel sorry for you that you that you wanted it so badly and didn't get it."

I glared at her. "Makayla, we—"

"Maybe you need to change your band name," she continued. "You could be the 'Almost Made It Girls.' Or the 'We Wish Girls.'" She cackled again before announcing, "Make sure you watch the six o'clock news tonight. Channel 9. That's when the ad runs for the first time."

"Channel 9?" someone at the next table asked.

"That's right," she answered.

"Six o'clock?"

"You know it," she answered. "But don't worry if you miss it. It's going to run, like, forty times a day or something, on every network."

As she strutted away, I mumbled, "I can't believe she's all fired up about everyone seeing her in some stupid tomato costume."

"She probably thinks she looks great in it," Mello said with a giggle. "I bet she's expecting everyone to copy her, like they always do."

"Now that *is* funny," I said. "Imagine all the Makayla followers wandering around school dressed in stuffed tomato suits."

Harmony laughed so hard her drink shot out her nose.

"And they can't fit into their desks!" I shrieked.

"Or through the classroom doors," Mello added.

That mental picture cheered me greatly. "Are we going to watch the ad together?" I asked.

"Definitely," Mello answered. "Let's meet at the shed. We can come early and practice for tomorrow."

• • •

As I tuned my electric, I thought about the song I'd been working on. "Are you up to trying something new?" I asked.

"Sí," Harmony answered, plucking out a pattern on bass.

Mello kept tapping on her snare. "What is it?"

I strummed a chord and began to sing the lyrics I'd written. After I finished, I asked, "So what do you think?"

"Love the beat," Mello answered.

"And the idea," Harmony added. "But it's missing something."

"Oh?"

"All that talk about being stronger—it sounds like it's all up to you," she explained.

Mello nodded. "Yeah. You don't mention *who* makes you strong. You sound really full of yourself—really proud."

"Whatever!" I said, tempted to put up my guitar and stomp out.

"Wait," Harmony insisted. "What if you added a line to the chorus after 'I'm gonna be tough enough to face the stuff that's poison in my mind. This time.' We could add, '*With God I'm stronger than I even know inside.*'"

"I like that," Mello said with a nod. "And on the second verse, after 'I'm gonna clean up the mess, endure the test,' add, 'Forget about my pride. This time, I'm stronger than I even know inside.'"

They looked at me hopefully. I looked back at them and said, "You make it sound like I have some serious issues or something. Do you think I'm proud?"

Both pairs of eyes dropped to the ground.

"What?" I asked. "What is this?"

"It's just that, with the way you've been acting about the talent show—" Harmony began, looking up.

Mello raised her eyes to mine. "It's like you have to prove yourself or something. Almost like your self-worth is based on how the talent show goes. Is something going on with you that we don't know about?"

"Forget it," I interrupted. "Just forget it. So we'll add those lines to the song, then." I played the intro. "Join in. Let's make some music."

Even with the new lines, the song rocked.

"Wanna do it tomorrow night?" Harmony asked.

Mello's face went pale. "At the talent show? We just learned it!"

"We perform new songs all the time," I reminded her. "Let's do it. It's perfect! *My* band signing the song *I* wrote at the show *I'm* in charge of. Ohwow!"

I couldn't wait to see Jake's reaction.

"You're doing it again, Trin," Mello said.

"Doing what?" I asked.

Harmony checked her phone. "Hold that thought! It's six o'clock. Get the TV on and let's check out the pepperoni princesses."

We squeezed onto the couch and sat through the opening news stories, anxious for the commercial break. "Do you really think they'll be dressed as different vegetables?" Mello asked.

"It fits, with restaurants trying to be healthier," I answered. "What mom wouldn't take her kid for pizza if it's being peddled by a singing tomato, a mushroom, and a green pepper? I'm *so* glad I heard about the costumes in time to get us out of it."

"Quiet! Commercials!" Harmony yelled.

The first few ads zipped by — car deals, furniture close-outs, new computers. And finally they were on: the Makayla Simmons band.

They looked stunning.

I couldn't match the awesome-looking band on the screen with the image I had worked up in my mind. "Where are the vegetables?" I asked.

I scooted closer to the television, as if I could make the costumes change by staring hard enough. It didn't work.

"Trin," Mello said, "they're wearing black pants and white tux shirts."

"And cute little fedora hats," Harmony added.

"Makayla looks awesome."

"They all do."

"Especially cute little Reesie!"

"They were supposed to look stupid."

"Why don't they look stupid, Trin?"

"I don't know, OK?" I asked. "I didn't pick the costumes."

"But you pulled us from the contest," Harmony reminded me. "You pulled us, because your stinking pride got you freaked about what we'd look like on TV."

"That could be us!" Mello added, pointing to the screen. "That *should* be us, singing on TV and looking good. We *so* had that deal in the bag."

The news came back on, and I got up to turn off the TV. I put my finger on the power button, but didn't push it.

"A local band is going big," the news anchor said. "The Makayla Simmons band, a group made up of females from Hopetown's James Moore school, recently won a regional contest sponsored by Pizza Pete's."

"I can't believe they're on the news!" I complained.

"Quiet!" Mello said.

"The new ad campaign will be aired on television stations in California, Arizona, Nevada, and Oregon. Channel 9's Gloria Guzman caught up with Makayla Simmons, the band's leader. Despite her busy schedule, Makayla took the time to answer a few questions for us."

"I bet she did!" I griped. "Like you had to beg her to be on TV."

"Quiet, Trin," Harmony whispered.

The screen showed Makayla, flipping her hair for the television audience, next to a tall woman with long black hair. "Makayla," the reporter said, "congratulations on winning this ad campaign. Is it exciting to see your band on television?"

"Yes, Gloria, it sure is!" Makayla gushed.

"So this must have been a busy week, trying to balance school and making a commercial."

Makayla's smile looked the closest to a real smile I'd ever seen from her. "It's been crazy, but it's been a lot of fun too."

"Now, am I right that you've also got a big part to play in your school's upcoming talent show?"

"What?" I yelled at the reporter. "She's nothing."

"I'm the director of choreography," Makayla said. "So we've had rehearsals all week, getting ready for tomorrow night. It's going to be a great show."

Gloria Guzman smiled into the camera. "There you have it. One of Hopetown's brightest and best. A young woman who can star in a commercial and coordinate her school's talent show all in the same week!"

I punched the power and the screen went black. "Coordinate her school's talent show? What was that?" I complained, turning my back on the television as if the machine itself were responsible for the outrage. "*I'm* coordinating the talent show. Makayla hasn't done anything except mess up a couple acts. I can't believe they interviewed *her* on the news! That so should have been me."

"And maybe it would have been, if you hadn't jerked us out of the contest," Harmony said.

I threw my hands up. "It's not my fault!"

"Yes, it is," she answered. "You've got some nerve, *amiga*! You just cost our band a huge opportunity. We could have made a ton of money. And the exposure! Four states, Trin. And all you're upset about is Makayla getting her name on the news instead of you."

"Not to mention the puke-green Makayla shirts we had to wear to school all week," Mello added, glaring at me. "All because of *you*. How hard would it have been to ask a few questions? Like, 'Excuse me, sir. What do the costumes look like?'"

I held my hands up. "You know what? I do *not* need this right now. I've got enough to be mad about without both of you attacking me."

"Then I guess we'll leave," Harmony said, standing up.

"Yeah," Mello agreed, following her to the door. "Let us know when you get over your injured pride. Then maybe you'll have time to think about the rest of us."

I crossed my arms as I watched them head out the door. Then I dug around until I found an old phone book. I got out my cell and dialed.

"Thank you for calling channel 9," the voice said. "How can I help you?"

"I'd like to correct a mistake in Gloria Guzman's report tonight," I answered. "I know your channel will probably send someone to the James Moore talent show tomorrow, and I want to be sure the reporter realizes that Trin Adams, *not* Makayla Simmons, has actually put the show together."

"*Trin* Adams? How do you spell that?"

I smiled. "T-R-I-N."

chapter • 11

...

Friday

Harmony and Mello didn't speak to me all day Friday. Neither did Harsha. Unfortunately, Makayla had plenty to say.

"Love the shirt," she called the second she spotted me in the hall. She caught up to me and walked right by my side, but she still talked loudly enough that I could have heard her if she'd been on a different floor. "That green is really working for you, Trin. It's so bright it reflects onto your face. Gives you an all-over greenish tint."

I cringed as I pushed my way through the crowded hall. Why couldn't she save her snotty comments for a time when less than two hundred people surrounded us? Or was that the whole point? I made myself smile and say, "Thanks. I've always liked green, myself."

"Or *is it* the shirt that makes your skin look green?" she asked, as if I hadn't responded. "Maybe the saying is true, and people actually turn green when they're jealous.

And you have so much to be jealous of, don't you? I'm sure you just wanted to die during dress rehearsal when Harsha called you down in front of the whole school! But I thought he was so gallant, coming to my defense like that."

"He is quite the gentleman," I agreed.

"Of course it may not be about Harsha at all. Did you see the ad last night?"

I took a deep breath. "I did."

"And?"

"You looked great. So did Reesie. Sounded great too," I told her.

Her face fell the tiniest bit. I guess she wanted me to say something rude so she could get a good fight going.

"Oh. Well, did you see my interview with Gloria Guzman?" she asked.

Now her words struck too close to home. I didn't know if I could trust myself to discuss that deceptive bit of "reporting" that had turned Makayla into the talent show coordinator. I raised my voice so it sounded as loud as hers. "That must have been exciting for you, Makayla. I can remember how thrilled I felt the first time I got on TV. Of course now it's no big deal."

She squinted angrily. "This was not my first—"

"Oh, look," I interrupted. "Here's my class. See ya later."

I knew I'd hear more from her, but I didn't have time to worry about it. Way too many details to deal with. Who cared about Makayla? In a few hours I'd be seeing my real father. I wondered if he would look the same as I remembered, and if he would be surprised to find *me* practically grown up.

•••

As the auditorium started to fill that night, I kept an eye on his seat. Front row, middle, just like I promised. I even taped a piece of paper there with his name in big, bold letters. I imagined him in that seat—right there, in front of me.

I thought about walking up to him after the show. In a soft voice I'd say, "Did you like it?" and he'd scoop me up and hold me high in the air, like he did when I was little.

"Like it?" he'd shout, smiling up at me. "I *loved* it! And I love you, Trin." Then he'd gather me into his arms. And I'd breathe in the spicy smell of his aftershave and feel like a little girl again, safe in the knowledge of my daddy's love.

"Trin, someone in Kelsey's group needs a safety pin," Latisha called.

"Got it," I answered, running for my emergency kit. I ran right into Lamont.

"What are you doing backstage?" I asked.

"Looking for you," he answered. "Let me do your pyrotechnics tonight, please. You've got way to much to think about, and—"

I rolled my eyes. "Oh, Lamont! It's so simple a five-year-old could do it."

"At least go over the instructions with me one more time," he begged.

"Trin!" Kelsey yelled. "Where's that safety pin?"

"Sorry, Lamont," I told him. "Gotta go. But don't worry! I can handle it."

I delivered the safety pin.

Harsha yelled, "Channel 9 is here!" The drill-team girls squealed and ran to the mirrors to add more makeup.

And clouds of hair spray that mingled with all the girls' flowery, fruity scents until backstage smelled just like a spa.

I helped Josephina fix the bow on her shirt, and hoped that receptionist for channel 9 had passed on my message. Tonight the news anchor would say, "Gloria Guzman caught up with the amazing Trin Adams, coordinator of the biggest and best talent show Hopetown has ever seen! Trin, we apologize for last night's erroneous statement about Makayla Simmons, who isn't anything like as important as you are."

"Channel 34 sent a camera crew!" Hunter called.

More squeals, more makeup, more hairspray.

I tried to get back onstage, in case someone wanted to interview me. But I couldn't even leave backstage, because so many people needed my help. Apparently, no one worried about me taking over tonight. Everywhere I turned, people begged me to do more.

I found someone's sheet music, helped Wesley glue a broken prop together, and assured a very worried Bentley that I wouldn't hide his keyboard from him. Finally, I got a chance to peek through the stage curtains and into the audience.

Jake's seat was still empty.

I felt my cell phone vibrating and thought, *Aha! Jake's probably lost on his way to the auditorium. I should have sent directions.*

I found my phone and opened it. Yep, a message from my father. I pulled it up.

Sorry, Trin. Something came up. Unable to make it to Hopetown this weekend. Will try to come soon. —Jake

I felt every heavy beat of my heart as I forced myself to read the words again. Not coming?

Jake wasn't coming.

Around me, everyone still rushed past with last-minute questions and instructions. "Trin, Jamie can't find her tap shoes!" "My earpiece isn't working!" "Where's Fatima's glove?"

Their voices and faces blended into a nervous blur—like an out-of-control spin on a merry-go-round.

I desperately wanted off.

Because suddenly, it had nothing to do with me. I didn't feel like part of the excitement anymore. I didn't care about the show.

I stood there like a statue, carved from stone. A statue with a big crack beginning at my heart and threatening to break completely in two.

When I could finally move, I started for the backstage door that led outside. By the time I reached it, I was running.

Outside, I threw myself onto the ground under the palm tree and let the crack in my heart rip me open. I pounded the springy green grass with my fists and cried—loud—until my throat hurt.

That's where Harmony and Mello found me.

"Trin?" Mello asked. "What on earth are you doing out here? The show's starting and—hey, are you crying?"

Harmony knelt beside me and threw her arms around me. "Trin! What's wrong? Did Makayla say something?"

The thought of Makayla and her rude comments seemed so small compared to the real problem, I laughed while I was still crying. "No," I managed to say, wiping my nose on my sleeve. "She didn't say anything."

"Then what is it?" Mello asked. Her voice was so sweet and sincere it brought my hurt right up to the surface. I started bawling again.

My friends waited patiently on either side of me —
Harmony holding my right hand and Mello holding my left.
And suddenly I knew I could trust them. Really trust them.
Even with my deepest, darkest secret.

I took a few long, shaky breaths. When I thought I could
control my voice I said, "My father promised to come tonight.
He *promised*. But he lied — again. He didn't come."

"Trin!" Harmony said, surprised. "He's in the front row!"
She tugged on my arm. I jumped to my feet, full of hope.
Jake came after all? Had the text message been some kind
of mistake?

"Silly Trin," Mello said as we walked to the door. "I can't
believe you didn't see him. He's sitting right next to your
mom."

I froze. "You mean Jeff."

"Well, duh," Harmony said. "Who else would we mean?
He's your dad, right?"

I felt the hot tears begin again. "He's my dad now. But he's
not my real dad."

"What?" Mello asked.

"My real father left Mom and me when I was four. I've
only seen him a few times since then. But I got a message
from him the other day. He said he wanted to see me, you
know? So I told him about the show, and he said he'd come.
And I believed him. I always believe him, because I hope —
maybe — maybe he'll change. Maybe he'll give me a chance."
I wiped angrily at the tears on my cheeks and whispered,
"Maybe he'll love me."

"Oh, Trin!" Mello cried. "You poor thing. I had no idea! I'm
so sorry."

Harmony's cheeks flamed red. "What a jerk! What kind of man makes promises like that and then—"

The door burst open and Latisha flew out. She looked us up and down before declaring, "Trin, I have no idea what kind of drama is going on out here, but the only show *I* know about is supposed to be *in there*." She turned and pointed dramatically to the auditorium. "Now, I know we've had our share of disagreements the past two weeks. I've told you in every conceivable way to back off. But right now, we're in the middle of the biggest event in the history of the school, and I need your help. Do you hear me, girlfriend? I am *desperate*! Props are disappearing, costumes are ripping, and cast members are freaking out and refusing to go onstage. If you don't hightail it in there right now, I'm gonna *personally make sure* you've got something to cry about."

Harmony and Mello stepped in front of me, forming a wall of protection.

"Don't you dare speak to Trin like that!" Harmony said, assuming her fighting stance.

Mello added, "You don't *even* know what she's going through right—"

"It's OK," I said, pushing the two of them apart so I could talk to Latisha. "You're right. I've worked too hard to let this show flop. Besides, it's nice to be needed."

Behind me, Harmony said, "But, Trin—"

I gave her and Mello a quick hug and said, "Thanks. We'll talk more later, OK?" Then I pasted on a smile and followed Latisha into the building. I had to pull the show—and myself—together.

...

chapter 12

Friday Night

Latisha hadn't exaggerated. Backstage was insane. In the few minutes I'd been gone, it seemed every conceivable problem had cropped up. I threw myself into helping, determined that even if Jake didn't see my show succeed, at least everyone in Hopetown would.

By the time Principal Fowler's lip-synch began, I felt utterly exhausted. But very pleased. The sound, the lights, the props, and yes—even the choreography—had all come together for each act. The response from the audience blew away what I had expected, or even hoped for. The show was a huge success.

I peeked through the curtain to watch Principal Fowler. I could hardly believe it. How could the man who danced around onstage pretending to sing a rock song be the same serious-looking principal who had called me to his office?

And I could see, in the audience, the same surprise on everyone else's faces. They loved it!

Another triumph.

"Trin!" Harmony said in a stage whisper. "We're next! You haven't even changed."

"Ohwow! I got so into everyone else's acts I forgot about ours," I admitted, grabbing my bag and following her and Mello to the backstage changing room. I pulled on my white fitted suit with the cross on it. "I'm glad we decided to wear the suits."

"They fit with the song," Harmony agreed, digging my boots out of the bag for me. "It's about God making us strong, and that's really what our super suits represent—how God makes us strong and works through us."

"Are you sure you're OK?" Mello asked, handing me a brush. "I mean, do you want to perform? We could back out, even now, if you don't feel up to it."

"No, let's do it," I told her. I had to look away from her probing eyes, or I knew I'd fall apart again. "We've got a great new song and an amazing backdrop that Wesley is setting up as we speak. I mean, it reeks that my father didn't show. But that doesn't mean everyone else should have to miss the best act of the night." We started jogging toward the stage. "Who knows? Maybe Jake will catch our act on TV."

Once we started the new song, it hit me how well it fit my situation. My voice sounded husky from crying, but that just added to the emotion I poured into each word:

Just when you've got the world inside your hand,
That's when nothing goes the way you planned.
You try and cry but still can't understand.

I'm gonna be stronger than the things I fight.
I'm gonna be stronger than the wrongs I right.
I'm gonna be tough enough to face the stuff
That's poison in my mind.

I watched the students rise to their feet. Then they opened their cell phones and waved them back and forth over their heads, and the glowing screens looked like little flames of hope all over the auditorium.

Flames!

I had forgotten to start the special effects!

During Mello's drum solo, I did a little grapevine step to the center of our backdrop. I found the small torch Lamont had told me to use. I looked at it and tried to remember what he'd said. Something about counting between each fuse I lit. But what was the number I needed to count to? Ten? Fifteen? I couldn't remember.

Anyway, Mello's solo would wrap up soon. It's not like she and Harmony could carry on while their lead singer and electric guitar player just hung out at the back of the stage, counting. Without me, the band had nothing.

I lit the fuses as fast as I could and danced my way back to my spot just in time for the second verse. I'm not sure it mattered that I made it back, though. Once the pyro started, the crowd went insane. They cheered so loud I'm sure they couldn't hear me sing.

Mello and Harmony looked as happy as I felt. I wanted to say, *"See? Didn't I tell you I could pull this off?"* But I could only tell them with my eyes as we kept playing.

I began the last verse, and my already scratchy voice almost broke as smoke started filling the stage.

Harmony coughed. I half turned and saw Mello blinking furiously. Behind her, a single plume of smoke rose. I looked harder and missed a few words when I understood why. Tiny yellow-orange flames licked at the base of a papier-mâché column! Not fireworks, but actual fire!

My heart beat in triple time as I spun the rest of the way around and faced the crowd. They swayed back and forth, singing our song. No doubt they thought the smoke came from a fog machine or something. Just more special effects. They had no idea about the disaster onstage.

And I planned to keep it that way.

I kept singing as I danced to the wings of the stage:

I'm gonna clean up the mess, endure the test.
Forget about my pride.

I put my mike behind me. "Latisha!" I hissed. "Get a fire extinguisher! Fast!"

I saw her eyes grow about four times larger before she turned and ran.

I picked up right where I'd left off on the song:

Sometimes it feels so hard just getting' through the day.
But that's not getting' in my way.

My mind raced as I freestyled through Harmony's bass solo. *Where is Latisha? And how can I put the fire out without anyone noticing?*

It all came down to this moment. The three thousand flyers, the huge poster that covered the front of the school, the Burma Shave signs. The visits and calls to TV and radio stations. The interclub meeting, the tryouts, the rehearsals. Even the papier-mâché backdrop and the pyrotechnics.

I'd done it all to convince everyone that I've got what it takes. To be known as Trin Adams—the person who transformed the James Moore talent show, and the whole school, into something to be proud of.

I didn't plan to let all my work go up in smoke.

I spotted Latisha in the wings, struggling with a huge bucket of water. A *bucket?* Where was the fire extinguisher?

Maybe I could grab the bucket and spin around, letting the water spray out behind me. The audience would think it was symbolic or deeply artistic. Whatever. I didn't care, as long as it saved our act.

But just as I grabbed the bucket, Mello saw the flames and screamed, "The set is on fire!" I wanted to stuff a sock in her mouth. What had happened to calm, reserved Mello?

It didn't help that her microphone broadcast her voice through the speakers. The audience went out-of-their heads crazy. People screamed and crowded the aisles, headed for the exits.

I realized there was no point singing anymore. Our act had capsized. But at least I could try to save the show.

I said into my mike as calmly as possible, "We're experiencing technical difficulties, ladies and gentlemen. Please return to your seats and remain calm."

It actually worked. They got quiet and sat back down.

Mello pulled her drums away from the flames. Harmony yelled, "Trin! A fire is not a technical difficulty! Are you *loco*?"

I ignored both of them and tossed the water on the fire. The flames went out, but it was too late. The automatic sprinkler system came on like a monsoon, raining huge drops of cold water on everything—us, our instruments, the backdrop.

Harsha and Hunter ran from the wings with fire extinguishers. "How did this happen?" Harsha demanded.

Hunter asked, "Are you OK, Trin?"

I didn't want to talk to them or even look at them. Especially when Makayla cackled out in the audience and called, "Great job, Trin! That's a really *hot* new song you've got there!"

I heard people laughing. But not Latisha. She stood in the wings, tears running down her cheeks.

Lamont ran onto the stage to help clear our equipment off. We handed guitars, monitors, drums, everything—to the people in the front row. Mom and Dad—I mean Jeff, of course—were right there helping. Lamont said, "Trin, I wish you had listened—" And that's when the world came crashing down. Okay, I guess it was really our huge backdrop. Weakened by the fire and then waterlogged, the two massive columns tipped like trees felled by an ax.

Makayla yelled, "Tim-ber!" as I leapt from the stage into Jeff's arms. He said, "I'm proud of you, Trin. I loved the show. And I love my girl!"

I felt huge tears threatening to spill over. "How can you say that?" I asked. "The whole thing's a disaster." I wrung water from my hair as I turned to look at what remained of my backdrop—a huge, nasty mess that covered most the stage. Jeff didn't say anything. He just put his arm around me.

The sprinklers stopped, and a fully recovered Latisha glided past the mess until she reached center stage. As if nothing out of the ordinary had happened, she said, "And now, ladies and gentlemen, our judges have completed their scoring. It's time to announce this year's winners."

I hated the thought of being around when the show ended. I didn't need to hear anyone's rude comments or funny jokes about our song. I desperately wanted to escape. "Let's go!" I whispered to my friends. I told my parents, "We'll be at the shed." Then we hunched over and sneaked through the back-stage area toward the back of the building.

I expected it to be dark outside, but as I pushed open the backstage door, I walked straight into a spotlight that almost blinded me.

"Trin Adams!" a familiar voice said. "You coordinated tonight's show, correct?"

I blinked, squinted, and struggled to figure out who was talking to me. When my eyes adjusted to the light I saw a tall woman with long black hair.

She said, "I'm Gloria Guzman here with a camera crew from channel 9, and I'd like to ask you a few questions about that unusually exciting finale we just saw!"

I panicked. Channel 9? Here? Now?

I ran my fingers over my stringy, wet hair and then wiped my bleary eyes, knowing drips of mascara must cover my cheeks.

So I finally got my interview, but not the one I'd planned on. Instead of the person who transformed her school into something to be proud of, I'd be interviewed on the news as the girl who caught the school on fire.

I shook my head, but it didn't matter. The reporter smiled and said, "Roll camera!"

chapter • 13

...

Later Friday Night

As soon as we were all in the shed with the door securely fastened, I started apologizing. "I'm sorry, everybody. I *so* wanted us to look good tonight."

"Us?" Mello asked. "Are you sure you were thinking of us—or did *you* want to look good tonight?"

I turned away. "Yeah. I guess you're right," I admitted. I sank into the couch and hid my face in my hands.

"Does this whole deal with your dad—I mean that other man—have anything to do with the way you've been acting lately?" Harmony asked, sitting next to me.

I shrugged.

"What are you talking about?" Lamont asked. "What other man?"

I blew out a huge breath. "I guess the word's out now. Jeff Adams isn't my real dad." I watched Lamont's face to see how he'd take the news.

His eyes got big. "What do you mean by *real* dad?" he asked.

"I mean, you know, my biological father. My dad now—Jeff—adopted me when I was seven. When he married my mom."

"So who's your real dad?" he asked.

"His name is Jake. He left Mom and me when I was really little."

Mello sat on a throw pillow on the floor in front of me. "Trin, why did you wait so long to tell us?"

"Lots of reasons. For one, you have perfect families—all of you," I answered. "I wanted you to think I did too."

Harmony snorted. "A perfect family? There's no such thing."

"You must not spend enough time at my house if you think we're perfect," Mello added.

"You know what I mean," I argued. "You each have your own mom and dad—still together. No steps. No divorce."

"You're embarrassed about the divorce?" Lamont asked. "You aren't responsible for the choices your parents made, Trin."

"Not embarrassed, exactly. I just wish it was different," I said, hugging a pillow to my chest. "Aren't dads supposed to love their kids? What was so wrong with me that my dad could walk away from me like that?" I felt the hot tears stinging my cheeks. "What's wrong with me *now*, that he still won't have anything to do with me?"

"Trin!" Harmony said, handing me a tissue. "There's nothing wrong with you, amiga. If he's not in your life, he's the one with problems."

Mello put her hands on my knees and gazed up at me. "He can't possibly know what he's missing. The poor man."

I blew my nose, and then I felt a grin spreading across my face. "Yeah, like tonight, for instance. Just think what he missed by not showing up like he promised."

"A show he'd not soon forget!" Harmony said with a giggle.

"He said he'd come to the talent show?" Lamont asked.

I nodded.

"So that's who the pyrotechnics were for?"

I nodded again. "And Makayla. And anyone else who thinks I'm a nobody, just 'the new girl who only sings in the Chosen Girls.'"

Harmony shook her head. "Trin! Tell me you *did not* let Makayla's stupid comment get to you."

I smiled a guilty smile. "I wanted to make a name for myself at James Moore."

"But, Trin," Mello argued, "you can't get your sense of worth from what other people think of you. If you do, there will always be someone around who can make you feel worthless."

"Well, I didn't get my self-worth just from what people thought of me," I said, running my hand through my hair.

"Oh?" Harmony asked, her eyebrows arched in disbelief.

"I also based it on what I could accomplish," I explained. "That's why the show had to be a smashing success."

Mello rolled her eyes. "Trin!"

"It always worked before," I admitted. "I can usually do whatever I decide to do."

Lamont nodded. "Now I get where that pride song came from."

"I've been reading a lot about pride lately," Harmony said. "Do you have a Bible out here, Mello?"

Mello handed an old children's Bible to Harmony, who flipped through the pages and then read, " 'Those who walk in pride he is able to humble.' That's Daniel 4:37."

"Ouch," Mello said.

"Do you think that's what happened tonight?" I asked. "That God used the show to humble me?"

"Do you feel humbled?" Harmony asked.

"Ohwow, yes," I answered.

"Then maybe so."

I noticed Mello stared hard at the clock on the wall.

"What's up, Mello?" I asked.

"It's ten o'clock," she said. "Do you want to watch the news?"

"Just in case I haven't been humbled enough?" I asked, standing up to flip it on. "I'm sure we'll hear about it forever. Might as well see it firsthand."

Gloria Guzman's face filled the television screen as she spoke into her microphone. "James Moore student Trin Adams promised a school talent show like we'd never seen before. Well, she delivered! Tonight's talent show was really smokin'!"

Gloria's commentary, which described the catastrophe in painful detail, continued as images of the smoke, confusion, and falling columns flashed on the screen. Then came my miserable interview.

"I look like a wet poodle!" I cried, horrified at the thought of people gathered around their televisions staring at my matted hair, blotchy face, and red eyes. I shook my head and listened to my voice saying, "Of course we didn't count on the fire. But all in all, it was a great show."

Gloria Guzman wrapped up the report with some quick coverage of Principal Fowler's act and the first place winner, Bentley, on the keyboard. It actually made the rest of the show sound decent. But by that point, I didn't care. I got up and turned the TV off. "Ohwow, that was beyond embarrassing," I said, flopping back onto the couch.

Harmony propped her feet up on the coffee table. "At least now the last two weeks make sense. I still can't believe you had this huge hurt you were dealing with and you didn't tell us."

"I guess I kind of like to pretend Dad—I mean Jeff—is my real dad. It seemed more believable here, because everyone just assumed it was true."

"I can see that. Did you say he adopted you when you were seven?" Mello asked.

"Yeah."

"And he's lived with you and your mom all the years since then?" Harmony asked.

"Well, yeah," I answered.

Lamont leaned back against the desk and crossed his arms. "Is he mean to you?"

I felt my jaw drop. "Mean to me? No!"

"Does he take care of you? Provide for you?"

"Of course. You know that, Lamont."

"Do you think he loves you?"

I couldn't figure out what Lamont was getting at. Irritated, I stood up and said, "I know he loves me. He just told me so tonight!"

Lamont got in my face. "Then you're being a jerk, Trin."

Harmony said, "Lamont!"

"Don't you think she's been through enough?" Mello asked.

My face felt like it was on fire, but I didn't want to back down. I looked Lamont in the eye and snarled, "What did you just say to me?"

His voice was softer, but strong as steel when he said, "What does Mr. Adams have to do before you'll count him as a 'real dad'?"

I stepped away from Lamont. My ragged breath tore through the silence of the room.

"You know what I mean," I whispered.

"Yeah, I know what you mean," he said. "But I also know that God has given you a gift. Mr. Adams is a godly man and a great father. He chose you, Trin. Maybe that other guy was stupid enough to walk away. So what? Mr. Adams got to know you, and he was smart enough to walk right into your life and stay there."

Lamont paced across the room and back, a bundle of pent-up energy. "Maybe Jeff Adams isn't your biological father, Trin, but he's as real a dad as you're gonna get down here. Quit selling him — and yourself — short."

"Do you have to be so aggressive, Lamont?" I asked.

He laughed. "Only when I'm talking to people as hard-headed as I am."

"Thanks, man," I said. "You're right. From now on, Jeff Adams is my *real* dad." I held my fist out to Lamont.

He bonked his fist against mine and bragged, "Of course I'm right! I'm always right!"

I looked at Harmony. "Could you read that verse from Daniel again? The one about those who walk in pride?"

"I hear ya," Lamont said with a grin.

"Know something cool?" Mello asked, stretching her long legs out in front of her.

I looked at her glowing face. "What?"

She smiled at me. "You've been adopted twice, Trin."

"Huh?"

Her eyes sparkled as she leaned toward me and said, "Jeff Adams isn't the only one who loved you so much he chose you to be his daughter. God chose you too. You know that."

I caught my breath as the beauty of being handpicked by God hit me in a fresh new way. "Ack. I'm going to cry again! How many tears can I produce in one day?" I asked, reaching for another tissue. "You're right, Mello, I already knew it, but . . . how did I forget? Thank you for reminding me."

She patted my leg. "Happy to do it. You're the one who taught me about being chosen by God, remember? Right here in the shed."

I looked around the room and thought back to that conversation with Mello. I had just moved to Hopetown, and just started to become friends with her, Harmony, and Lamont. Now I couldn't imagine life without the three of them.

"God's been so good to me!" I said, overcome. "He's given me the best friends anyone ever had. And he loves me. *God loves me!* Ohwow! It's way fabulous, isn't it?"

"Doesn't get any better," Harmony agreed. "If you're looking for a reason to feel good about yourself, Trin, I don't think you need to look any further."

Someone pounded on the door, and we all jumped.

"Who could that be?" I asked. "We're all here."

Mello opened the door.

"Latisha!" she said in surprise.

My heart jumped to my throat.

"Sorry to barge in on you," Latisha said as she stepped into the room. "But I've been everywhere looking for—" She spotted me on the couch. "Trin! I tried the Java Joint first, and then I went to your house. They sent me to Mello's, and her parents sent me here."

"You could have called," I suggested, holding up my cell. I hadn't planned on facing Latisha yet.

She crossed her arms and said, "Oh, no. I wanted to look you in the eye for this. All I have to say is—"

I didn't want to get yelled at, so I took a deep breath, stood up, and interrupted her. "I'm sorry, Latisha. I've been a total pain from the word *go*."

"That's true," she agreed.

I bit my lip then held my fingers up as I numbered my offenses. "One, I tried to prove my worth by creating an awesome talent show. Stupid idea. Totally backfired. Two, I took over your job—"

"And everyone else's," she added

I nodded. "And everyone else's, as if I could do it all. I was full of pride, and I found out the hard way God's not into that."

Latisha stood there, arms crossed, staring at me.

I stared back.

"Is that all?" she asked.

"I spent too much on publicity," I answered.

"And?"

"Well, of course, I caught the stage on fire and then soaked it."

"And?"

I wiped away the sweat beading up on my forehead. "Um—I didn't stay to clean up."

"And?"

I searched my memory. "That's all I can think of at the moment," I answered.

"Then let me tell you what else you did, Trin Adams. It's the real reason I've been all over town looking for you," she said. She stepped closer to me and pointed her finger at my chest.

"You did exactly what you promised to do. You revolution-ized the James Moore talent show. The school—no, the whole town—is talking about it. The acts were amazing. The turnout was fabulous. And ticket sales, like you promised, more than covered publicity and a large pepperoni pizza for Bentley, who, by the way, doesn't belong to a club. The student council ended up with more money than we've had in the history of the school. That's why I had to find you, Trin. To say thanks."

I laughed in surprise. "But, Latisha, my grand finale was a disaster!"

"You know that's right," she agreed. "But that was one tiny part of the evening, Trin. Four or five minutes, maybe. Everything else turned out great." She smiled as she crossed her arms again. "Did you think this whole night was about you?"

"Ouch. I hear you," I said with a nod.

She headed for the door. "By the way, don't worry too much about the fallout over the whole fire thing. Everyone knows the Chosen Girls rock, and everyone knows you pretty much single-handedly turned the show around. Not that you won't hear a few jokes about it now and then—how you really 'lit up the stage' is my favorite. Or that next week you guys are 'burning a new CD.' Or there's the one about—"

"That's probably enough for tonight," I said, playfully shoving her outside. "See ya Monday."

I closed the door and turned around to face Mello, Harmony, and Lamont. They all had their hands over their mouths, shaking with laughter.

"Well, Trin, your dream came true after all," Mello said between giggles.

Harmony nodded. "You've definitely made a name for yourself at James Moore. And I hate to bring it up, because I'm sure you're still a little sensitive about the topic of fire, but—"

"What?"

She and Mello held up their green Makayla Simmons shirts. "We need to start just one more small fire tonight!" Mello said with a smile.

chapter • 1

...

Friday night

I sing alto—even when I'm alone. I'm just not a "lead singer" kind of person. Never have been.

Okay, that's not totally true. I used to start songs on family car trips—back in grade school. We always took Harmony with us so I'd have someone to play with. So I'd start a song and Harmony would join in.

But she'd start at a different part of the song. Not because she wasn't musical. Despite her voice (which isn't too hot), Harmony was born to make music. I think she did it just to see if I'd follow her lead.

There we were in the backseat of the Ford—me singing and her singing, but not together. It didn't match, and it made me crazy. I'd hold out for as long as I could, waiting for her to catch up or slow down, but she never did. Finally, I'd give up

I'd be mad about it for hours, but I would do it. Because it was easier than fighting.

Maybe all friendships are like that—with a leader and a follower. It doesn't really bug me, but sometimes I wonder what leading would be like—especially since Trin moved here and even bosses Harmony. You know, what would it be like—to be the leader for once?

• • •

Harmony and I crowded around the tiny bathroom mirror. "Mello, remember to have fun onstage," Harmony said, slapping powder on her nose. "Everyone here loves us."

Trin pushed between us and eyed me in the mirror. "Yeah, Mello. There's no reason why even *you* should be nervous tonight!"

"I'll *get* nervous if you make some huge issue out of it," I said, fluffing my hair one last time. "I so wish he didn't have to interview us."

Trin smeared gloss over her perfect lips and then smiled at her reflection. "I love interviews. It's way fabulous to think so many people actually care about what I have to say!"

"*Sí*," Harmony agreed. "It's cool frijoles making everyone laugh, you know? Feels almost as good as making music." She frowned at me. "Why can't you get used to interviews, Mello?"

I dug a lip gloss out of Trin's bag. "Spouting answers off the top of my head is torture. I like to actually *think* before I speak."

Harmony laughed. "Ooh! Was that a slam on us, Trin?"

I looked in the mirror and saw my cheeks turn red. "No!" I said. "I didn't mean—"

"I know you didn't," Harmony interrupted, pulling me to the door. "I forgive you anyway."

Trin stayed at the mirror. She moved one strand of hair three more times before I yelled, "Trin, your hair was perfect, as always, before we even came in here. Come on!"

We raced past huge inflatables of every color, size, and shape where people—even teens and adults—jumped, climbed, screamed, and laughed. As we neared the small temporary stage near the front entrance Trin asked, "Why are we running? It's not like they can start without us. It's our party!"

Harmony said, "*No se.* Why *are* we running?"

"Because we're psyched," I told them. "And we're scared of Mr. Jacobs."

They nodded in agreement as we leaped up the steps. I slipped behind my drum set and they fine-tuned their guitars.

Then Mr. Jacobs stepped to the mike. The music stopped and his strong voice filled the building. "Please, everyone, gather around the stage area."

The floor around us got crowded right away. People can't help but obey Mr. Jacobs.

"We're all here tonight to celebrate a special occasion," he said. "The Chosen Girls are an amazing group. It's been fun to watch their rise to stardom, and I'm pleased that my company has been blessed with the opportunity to produce their first full-length CD." He paused while everyone cheered. "They're going to play a song for us, and then we'll ask them a few questions. Chosen Girls, take it away!"

I couldn't stop smiling as I played my drums and sang. It was maybe the most fun I've ever had performing, because I didn't feel any pressure. My friends were right. I looked at the people in the audience—my family, Trin's family, Harmony's family. All our friends *and* every boy we'd ever had a crush on. They made up the smallest crowd we'd performed in front of in a long time, but they couldn't have been louder or more energized if there had been thousands.

Besides, the longer we played, the longer we put off the interview.

My good feelings wore off the moment Mr. Jacobs made us come up to the front of the stage for the interview. I like to "hide behind my drums," as Trin and Harmony say.

Still, it started off okay. The mike bounced between Trin and Harmony, whose answers sounded as professional and polished as any talk-show host's. I just stood quietly to the side, reminding myself to keep smiling.

Then Mr. Jacobs said, "Mello, you haven't had an opportunity to share. Why don't you answer that one?"

Harmony gave me the mike and an encouraging smile.

Without moving my smiling lips, I whispered, "Harmony, what was the question?"

"School," she hinted.

What about school?

I smiled at Mr. Jacobs and said, "Um, we all three go to James Moore. And our sound man and videographer, Lamont, is homeschooled."

Mr. Jacobs's smile seemed to grow icy. "Yes, Mello, Trin just told us that. I asked you whether you're in any extracurricular activities at school."

"Oh!" I exclaimed. "Um, yes—"

Harmony grabbed the mike. "We're all superinvolved at James Moore. Mello and I are on yearbook and ..."

I wanted to crawl under the stage and cry as Harmony's voice droned on and on. It's not like the question was too hard for me. I wasn't ready for it, that's all.

Mr. Jacobs didn't call on me again, so I guess that was one good thing about flubbing the answer. I went back to standing quietly to the side and reminding myself to smile, which took a ton more work than it had before.

As soon as he started wrapping up, I took a step backward. Then the minute the interview ended, I flew to the break room where we'd put our junk. It seemed like a good place to hide, and I hoped no one would notice that I was missing.

They didn't. And why would they? Trin and Harmony are the dazzling ones, the ones everyone loves to be around. They always know what to say and when. Usually I'm proud of them, but sometimes they make me crazy — like tonight during the interview.

I crossed my arms and meandered around the break room, looking for anything to take my mind off what a fool I'd made of myself. I knew I'd have to get back to the fans before long, but I wasn't ready. So I read safety notices and employee-of-the-month posters tacked to the wall, and I enjoyed being alone.

A cooler on the floor had a note taped to it: "Help yourself." I lifted the lid and saw a few sodas floating in icy water. I recognized a black and red can as one of those energy drinks. *That might help*, I thought as I dipped my hand into the freezing water and pulled out the drink. *If I had more energy, maybe I'd be more like Trin and Harmony.*

I popped the lid and took a swig. *Ew! Too sweet. Should have chosen Coke instead,* I thought. But the cold liquid felt good on my throat, and I hated to waste it, so I forced the rest down. I'd just tossed the empty can into the trash with a *clunk* when the door burst open.

"Mello, what are you doing in here? Come do the bungee run with us!" Harmony yelled. "Lamont's got his camera ready."

I walked to the door, and she and Trin grabbed my hands and rushed me through the crowd of celebrating people. I tried to calm down by humming along with the music that blasted out of the speakers, filling the huge building. The song was "You've Chosen Me," from our newly released CD.

We got stopped at least ten times before we made it to the huge red inflatable.

"Congratulations!"

"Great job!"

"You sound amazing!"

Lamont met us at the bungee run. It looked something like two connected bowling lanes made from massive air-filled pillows. It stretched thirty feet long and fifteen feet wide with a back wall that must have been three times taller than me. Still, it wasn't close to being the largest inflatable in the building.

Trin handed me a helmet.

I hesitated. "A helmet for a bounce house?"

Harmony laughed and pointed to the massive inflatable. "This is not your old-fashioned birthday party bounce house. Trust me, you want the—"

"Hello?" I said, trying to give the thing back to Trin. "Helmets are designed to protect the skull from being crushed. I'm so not into anything that can crush my skull."

Trin pushed the helmet back at me. "Come on, Mello. No wimps allowed tonight. You're a rock star and a superhero! Act like it, for once."

I crossed my arms. "For once? Whatever, Trin."

"Oh, don't go dramatic," she said, rolling her eyes. "You know what I mean, Mello."

Harmony grabbed the helmet, put it on my head, and adjusted the straps. "The bungee run is major fun-o-rama. And I promise you'll be fine."

"I hope so," I answered. "I guess I'll make the best of it, since you two are going to make me do it no matter what I say."

Harmony patted the top of my helmet and smiled. "Sí! That's the spirit."

"Exactly right!" Trin said, taking my hand and helping me onto the blown-up runway. At the far end, she showed me how to snap on the harness that connected to the back wall.

I felt my heart beat faster, partly from being nervous but mostly from excitement. *And maybe*, I thought, *from that energy drink I just had. Wow!*

"Are all CD release parties this cool?" I asked Lamont.

"I don't know," he answered. "First time I've heard of one at a warehouse full of inflatable obstacle courses and slides and stuff, but hey, it works for me."

"Ohwow, yes," Trin agreed, bouncing away from me. "This place is a blast."

In the lane next to mine, Harmony checked her own harness. "I *hope* they're all this fun. We're booked solid for the next month."

"I thought recording the CD was the hard part," Lamont said. "Who knew the real work is promoting it?"

"OK. Ready?" Trin called from her spot on the floor. She pointed to a small flag resting on the air-filled wall that divided my lane from Harmony's. "I'll count down and you both race for the flag. The person who grabs it first, wins. And you have to run hard, Mello. No half-hearted jogging."

Half-hearted? Why did she think I'd be half-hearted?

Trin counted — "three, two, one" — and I ran for the flag. Just as I reached out, Harmony swiped it and then — *oof!* My bungee cord snapped me back. I flew through the air for a few feet before I crashed into the puffy wall behind me.

I laughed in surprise. I could hear Harmony's deep laughter, but I couldn't see her because she had snapped back too. Someone cheered, and I scrambled up to see Karson and the guys from his band at the end of the run. Karson yelled, "Wow, Mello. That super suit you're wearing totally works — you can fly!"

"You know it!" Lamont crooned. "I got some serious flight-time action shots. All I have to do is run this in reverse and change the background. Wah-lah! The Chosen Girls are cruising the skies in their next music video."

"Give me a copy of it as soon as you get it ready," I told him, rubbing my sore neck. "I've always wanted to fly, but I'd so rather do it on tape. Less painful."

Trin bounded down the lane to help me unclip the harness. "Oh, quit whining," she said as I pulled off the helmet. "See? Your skull is intact, just like we promised."

I followed her back toward the front of the lane and solid ground. Karson reached for my hand to help me down. Instead, I handed him the helmet.

"Here," I said. "I want to see you do it."

He grinned that lopsided grin that makes it so hard for me to breathe. "Sure. Cole, get Harmony's helmet. I'll take you on."

I sighed with relief. I'd managed to say something to Karson that didn't make me sound stupid. And when Karson beat Cole to the flag, I cheered like he had won a gold medal at the Olympics.

Cole wanted a rematch. Karson asked, "Are you sure you want me to embarrass you again?"

Hunter jumped onto Cole's lane. "Sorry, loser. My turn. I'll show Karson how it's done."

"Good luck!" Karson spouted back. "I'm the Bungee King."

Must be nice to be so confident. But as I looked at Karson's shiny brown curls and sparkling eyes I thought, *Of course he's confident. All that talent and the good looks too.*

"Quit staring," Trin whispered.

"I'm just watching the race!" I answered, offended.

She tugged my elbow. "I know. Just teasing. But let's do something else. There's a boxing ring over there with huge blow-up boxing gloves."

"I so have to see you two box each other," Harmony said with a laugh. She grabbed my other elbow and steered me toward the boxing ring.

"So, having fun now that the interview is over?" Trin asked.

"Yeah. About that interview, Harmony. School? What kind of lame hint was that?"

"Hey, I tried," she answered, throwing her hands up. "You could listen, you know."

Trin joined in. "Really, Mello. Not being able to come up with an answer is one thing. But not even knowing the question?"

Chosen Girls is a dynamic new series that communicates a message of empowerment and hope to Christian youth who want to live out their faith. These courageous and compelling girls stand for their beliefs and encourage others to do the same. When their cross-cultural outreach band takes off, Trinity, Melody, and Harmony explode onto the scene with style, hot music, and genuine, age-relatable content.

Backstage Pass
Book One • Softcover • ISBN 0-310-71267-X

In *Backstage Pass*, shy, reserved Melody gets her world rocked when a new girl moves in across the street from her best friend, Harmony. Soon downtime—or any time with Harmony at all—looks like a thing of the past as the strong-willed Trinity invades Melody and Harmony's world and insists that the three start a rock band.

Available now at your local bookstore!

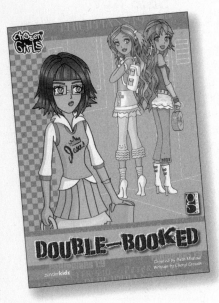
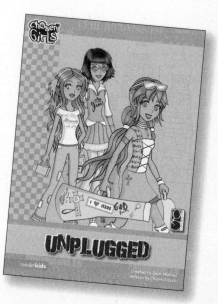

Solo Act

Book Four • Softcover • ISBN 0-310-71270-X

Melody needs some downtime—and
the summer youth retreat will really
hit the spot! But a last-minute crisis at
camp means an opportunity for the
band to lead worship every morning,
plus headline the camp's big beach
concert and go to camp for free. Too
busy and unhappy, Melody makes some
selfish choices that result in the girls
getting lost, sunburned, in trouble, and
embarrassed. Can she pull out of
the downward spiral before she ruins
camp—and the band—completely?

Big Break

Book Five • Softcover • ISBN 0-310-71271-8

The Chosen Girls are back! As
opportunities for the band continue to
grow, Harmony can't resist what she sees
as a big break ... and what could be better
than getting signed by an agent?

Available now at your local bookstore!

Overload

Book Seven • Softcover • ISBN 0-310-71273-4

Melody discovers a latent talent for leadership that she never knew she had. When she begins a grief recovery group for kids like her, she loses her focus on the work God is doing through the Chosen Girls.

Reality Tour

Book Eight • Softcover • ISBN 0-310-71274-2

When the Chosen Girls go on their first multi-city tour in a borrowed RV, Harmony's messiness almost spoils their final show. What's worse, she almost blows her opportunity to witness to her cousin Lucinda.

We want to hear from you. Please send your comments
about this book to us in care of zreview@zondervan.com. Thank you.